They had exact[ly] [...] abandon the statio[n] [...] of orbit before the alien space[craft] on top of them. If the aliens were true to form, they'd drain the energy from this place. If Banks and her crew stayed, they would die here. Their air would run out first or they'd freeze to death.

She wasn't going to die that way.

None of them were.

Making sure everyone was ahead of her, she gave one quick glance around the control room, then reached down and keyed in one last command.

The computers would track the incoming ships. When they were almost close enough to drain the energy from the station, it would explode with enough hydrogen bombs to level half of Europe.

The ISS had become just another weapon in the many that Earth would be throwing at the aliens this time. But if the ISS took out even one alien ship, it would be worth it.

Quickly she headed behind her crew toward the shuttle. Twelve minutes to board, release from the station, and drop into the atmosphere. No one had ever done that in under an hour before.

But they would.

They had to.

They had no other choice except death . . .

By Dean Wesley Smith and Kristine Kathryn Rusch
Published by The Ballantine Publishing Group:

THE TENTH PLANET
THE TENTH PLANET: OBLIVION
THE TENTH PLANET: FINAL ASSAULT

THE TENTH PLANET FINAL ASSAULT

Dean Wesley Smith and Kristine Kathryn Rusch

Story by Rand Marlis and Christopher Weaver

A Del Rey® Book
THE BALLANTINE PUBLISHING GROUP • NEW YORK

A Del Rey® Book
Published by The Ballantine Publishing Group
Copyright © 2000 by Creative Licensing Corporation and Media Technologies Ltd.

www.randomhouse.com/delrey/

Library of Congress Catalog Card Number: 00-107309

ISBN 0-345-42142-6

Manufactured in the United States of America

First Edition: December 2000

10 9 8 7 6 5 4 3 2 1

To Brent and Stephanie,
who were there when it all began.

Section One

PANIC

1

October 11, 2018
7:04 P.M. Central Daylight Time

30 Days Until Second Harvest

The ancient El train shuddered to a stop. Kara Willis grabbed the metal bar to keep herself from being flung into the man next to her. His overalls smelled of grease and onions, and his hands were filthy. He obviously had some kind of job that required maintenance work. This was not her crowd, from the tired, overweight women who clutched large purses against their old overcoats to the men with haggard faces and exhausted eyes. They made her uneasy.

A garbled announcement sounded around her. She made out "tracks" and "closed" and "wait." The announcement was repeated in Spanish, and the words were much clearer. But even though she was in her third year of high school Spanish, she could only make out a few words. Most of them were extremely unfamiliar.

Around her the crowd groaned.

"What was it?" she asked the man beside her.

He blinked, his eyes blue and red-rimmed. "Trouble down the tracks. They're closing this line. They suggest waiting for a different train."

"Which one?" she asked.

But he just looked at her, and shook his head slightly.

"Probably better to walk, *niña*," the woman across from her said.

Kara's eyes widened. She couldn't walk. They had stopped at Superior and State, right downtown, and she lived in Lake Forest. Walking was not an option, and from what she'd seen through the scratched and dirty windows the last half hour, she knew she wouldn't find a cab.

It was her fault. Her friends had driven her home from school, the BurpeeKins blaring on the CD player, so she hadn't been prepared for what she found when she got to the house.

Her mom had been sitting on the couch, hands in front of her face, shoulders shaking.

The wall screen had been pulled down and ten channels appeared on it, all of them with the volume on, so that a bunch of voices blasted her. The newscasters, usually sprayed and combed to perfection, looked frazzled. On the screen below them or above them were the words "Breaking News," and a few of the images showed a round blackness coming around the sun.

She recognized that image—she had seen it enough

4

since the president's speech last summer. It was the tenth planet, and it was coming back toward them.

The first time it had come, it had destroyed various areas all over the Earth. One of them had been in California, where her cousin Barbara had lived. She had gone to the memorial service that her grandparents and aunt and uncle had held for Barbara. There hadn't been anything left of her cousin. Someone had had to go to court in California and have Barbara—and everyone who had lived in the ruined areas of Monterey—declared legally dead.

Kara's mother didn't even seem to notice that she was home. Kara put her purse on the couch and picked up the remote. Her mother continued to shake. For a moment, Kara put her hand over her mom's frail back, then pulled away. She had not seen her mom like this, not since the aliens had attacked the first time.

Kara muted nine channels, leaving only the handsome guy from CNN. Only he wasn't so handsome now. He looked as upset as her mom, except that he didn't have the luxury of burying his face in his hands.

The aliens had launched a new fleet of ships at Earth. They were going to attack again.

Her father came out of his office at that moment, his feet bare, his hair tousled. He looked like a man who had been punched in the stomach.

"Turn it off, Kara," he said.

Her mother lifted her head. "No—"

He grabbed the remote and shut off the entire screen. "There's nothing we can do," he said. "This time, we're all going to die."

"But we attacked them," Kara said. "We bombed them with every nuke on the planet. We won."

"They're more powerful than we are," her mom said. "They can survive anything."

Kara's father met her gaze. His dark eyes were sad.

"I'm so sorry, honey," he said to her, and then dropped on the couch and put his arm around her mom.

Maybe it was his apology that made her leave.

Or maybe it was her mom's shuddery "What are we going to do?"

Or maybe it was pure fear.

Whatever it was drove her out of the house, down the lawn and into the street.

Inside all the other houses, people were standing or shouting or shaking their heads. But no one else had come outside. She needed company—and not her parents. Her father's look had said too much, just as he had said too much last April.

If we had known this was going to happen, she had overheard him saying to a friend, *we never would have brought a child into this world.*

And then, that afternoon, *I'm sorry, honey.* Not for going to her mother instead of her, but for bringing her into a world with no hope.

She had run down the street, fists clenched. There was nothing she could do, but she felt like she had to do something. She didn't want to sit around and calmly wait for death.

Somehow that impulse had brought her out of her neighborhood to the El. She had gotten on, thinking she would go somewhere else, where people stood out-

6

side and stared at the sky, where they were discussing the future instead of cowering inside their homes.

Instead, her impulse had turned into a long, nightmarish trip on the El. The people on the train looked tired and sad. They had been hopeless even before the aliens had come.

And then the train went through neighborhoods she had never been in alone.

As she looked through the scarred windows, she saw people flooding the streets, but they weren't people she wanted to mix with. These people were angry. They were breaking windows and shaking fists at the sky. At one intersection, she saw boys younger than her carrying beer out of a liquor store—through the shattered windows.

Then, as the sun set, an orange glow filled the skyline. The glow hadn't come from the fall sun. It looked unnatural. One of the men farther down in the El car had said, "Fire!" and everyone had looked, heads moving in unison!

Just as quickly, they looked away, pretending to see nothing, shoulders huddling inward, trying to keep as much personal space between them as possible.

"*Niña*." The kind woman across from Kara had touched her shoulder, shaking her out of the memory. "They do not want us on this train."

Kara stood. She gripped the metal bar tightly and wondered what she was going to do. She had planned to ride to the Loop, change trains and go home. But this train was stopping before they got to the Loop, and now they were making her get off.

Passengers filed off the train in an orderly fashion, looking as defeated as her father had. She had run, but there had been nowhere to go.

She hadn't realized until just a few hours ago that she was trapped here—not in this train, this neighborhood, not in Chicago, but on Earth.

Suddenly the world seemed very, very small.

Her eyes burned. No wonder her mother was crying. No wonder people cowered in their houses. They had already figured out that there was nowhere to go.

As she stepped onto the platform, she saw a chubby man in a blue Chicago Transit Authority uniform guide the flow of people down the stairs. There were other CTA employees scattered along the track, most of them looking tense. It wasn't the kind of tense she would have expected—not the kind she was feeling. It was a more immediate thing, as if they were expecting her—or someone—to jump them.

She followed the people down the stairs, their feet making rumbling sounds as they went. In the distance, she heard shouting and screaming and gunshots. The air smelled of smoke. She shivered. She hadn't even remembered to bring a jacket.

She crossed to the other side and started up the stairs so that she could catch a train home—or at least back in the direction she had come—but another CTA employee, a man with lined features, a man who looked as old as her father, put his hand on her shoulder.

"Sorry," he said. "This line's closed."

"I've got to go home," she said.

He shook his head. "There won't be any trains on this track all night. Maybe not even tomorrow."

She glanced over her shoulder. The tall buildings of downtown were only a few blocks away. "Where's the next nearest station?"

He looked down at her and seemed to see her for the first time. People were flowing around them, walking down more steps to the street level. Another gunshot echoed, this time even closer, followed by the sound of breaking glass.

"You'd have to walk," he said. "And I can't guarantee that any of the other trains will be running."

She felt panic surge through her, panic she had been controlling until now. "Why not?"

He glanced over his shoulder. "The entire city's gone nuts. I don't think it's safe to be on the streets. Where are your parents? Maybe they should come get you."

She wasn't even sure that her parents knew she was gone. They probably thought she was cowering in her room. "I'll walk," she said. "Just point me in the right direction."

"Look." He put a hand on her arm. "I have a booth upstairs. You can wait there until your parents come. It'll be safer."

She would have taken him up on that a year ago. Maybe even six months ago, when the aliens first attacked. She had still believed then that, despite the disaster, life would continue.

Now she was sure she was going to die. It was just a question of when.

She shrugged herself out of his grasp. "I'll be all right," she said, and hurried down the stairs. He called after her, but she ignored him. Her heart was pounding and her mouth was dry. As she stepped onto the street, she saw a group of men push a car over. It looked like someone was still inside it.

More glass broke, and people carrying boxes ran past her.

The smoke wasn't as thick here, but the air smelled funny—of sweat and piss and something else, something that made the hair on the back of her neck rise. Maybe that was what fear smelled like?

Men sat on the curbs, head in hands, just like her mother had done.

Women watched from windows as children and teenagers ran wild in the street.

No one was making any effort to stop the mayhem.

No one really seemed to notice except her.

And part of her wanted to join in. It seemed logical somehow. Why wait for the aliens? What did they want anyway? To destroy the Earth. Why not destroy it before they did, make sure there was nothing left for them to touch?

Because when the aliens had come the first time, they had sent down a cloud of blackness that had eaten through everything—including people. She had seen those scenes of people being devoured alive. Her father had tried to steer her away from the TV, but she had seen it anyway. And then they had learned that her cousin Barbara—her skinny, obnoxious, giggly cousin—had died in the last attack.

Melted, eaten alive, just like everyone else.

And it had looked so painful.

Kara didn't want to die. She didn't want to die that way.

Behind her something banged so loud that she felt the ground shudder. She turned around. Another car had overturned, this one the size of her family's sedan. Kids her own age were jumping on it, screaming at the person inside as if they blamed him.

Maybe they should blame him. Maybe they should blame all the grown-ups. After all, they had lied. Every one of them, from the president on down, had lied. They had said, when we bombed the tenth planet, that the Earth had won.

And it hadn't. It hadn't at all.

Now the aliens were coming back, probably angrier and meaner. Maybe they would be like the creatures in those bad SF flat movies her teacher had shown in history class, the ones that showed all the paranoia of the last century. Those aliens had always gotten stronger after they were bombed.

Kara shuddered. She pressed herself against the cold brick wall of a nearby building and watched the destruction around her. She couldn't walk from here, and she didn't want to go back to the El.

She didn't really want to go home either.

There was nothing left for her. She had a month left to live—the whole world had a month left to live—and she was only seventeen years old.

Her dad had been right. It wasn't fair. She deserved a future.

11

The president promised that the Earth would defend itself and survive, but that was a lie, too.

She sank down onto the filthy sidewalk. No matter what she did tonight, it would make no difference thirty days from now.

Thirty days from now, she would be dead, and there would be no one around to notice, no one to remember her, and no one to care.

October 11, 2018
19:13 Universal Time

30 Days Until Second Harvest

General Gail Banks never grew tired of the view from orbit. Spread out below her the whites, browns, blues of Earth seemed intense and alive. From this distance, her home seemed so small and vulnerable. Hard to believe there were nearly ten billion lives on it, all of them important, all of them connected.

And all of them in her care.

She touched the round frame of the portal in her tiny office on the International Space Station. In the last few months, this place had also become home to her. A cobbled-together home, filled with quirky, competent people, all as determined as she was to save that beautiful blue ball below her.

She had coordinated the missile attack on the tenth planet from this station. She had been pleased that they had managed to arm and send over three hundred missiles at the tenth planet.

The aliens had destroyed most of the missiles, but at least fifteen had gotten through.

Her readings here had shown that the damage to the tenth planet had been severe. She had also known that the aliens hadn't been obliterated, even though the word on the vid news and the Net among the civilians was that Earth had "won" the war.

Earth had won a battle, and that was all.

She had spent the last few months making certain that Earth would be able to defend herself in the coming battle.

She wanted Earth to win the war—and she knew now she had a month to make it happen.

She leaned her forehead against the cool plastic wall. If any of her subordinates saw her, they would be shocked. To them, General Gail Banks was coldly professional, heartless and probably soulless, a woman who demanded not just perfection, but complete dedication to the task at hand.

Here, though, in the privacy of her small cubicle, she allowed herself to feel the disappointment that had been welling inside her ever since she had seen the video of the alien ships being launched from the strange dark planet.

The ships were visible only as bright flares against the planet's black surface. All of the telescopes had recorded the images, and she had received them on a scrambled channel. Flares, like fireflies against a moonless night sky. Impossible for her to tell exactly how many there were, but she knew there would be enough to destroy much of Earth.

If she failed to stop some of them.

She wouldn't fail.

She stood up straight and sighed, looking at Earth again. The cool blue oceans, the clouds thin as gauze, the browns and greens of the land. From the International Space Station, Earth itself seemed like little more than an island, a small oasis in the vast ocean of the universe.

Those aliens would have to come through her: General Gail Banks, the heartless soulless perfectionist who loved the Earth more than she loved her country, perhaps more than she loved herself. Perhaps her troops saw that. Perhaps that was why no one had transferred, even when they learned as much as they could about the mission.

They believed that with her leadership, they would get the job done.

If she survived the battle against the aliens, it would be because of a miracle, some unexpected miracle that no one could have predicted. She was going to die in this plastic junk-heap, die defending that beautiful blue ball below, and she was proud that she was going to die this way.

She had always hoped that she would die in battle. She had expected to die in some border skirmish, directing troops for the U.S. But she wasn't going to die in some minor war. She was going to die in the greatest battle in this planet's history, the battle that would determine if the planet *had* a history, the battle that would determine if there would be someone left to remember the history.

She knew nothing about the aliens, except that they had attacked the Earth for no reason, and that they were difficult to destroy. In their position, she would be angry—a general of a dominant power who had lost an unexpected battle and been attacked on the home front. But she didn't know if these creatures felt anger.

She didn't know if they felt anything at all.

For the first time in human memory, the enemy was a cipher, something impossible to understand. And, surprisingly, she wished she had the power to understand them. Then she could predict their actions. She wasn't sure if they were coming back to repeat the same attack they had made before, or if they were going to do something different. If she had an understanding of them, an emotional reading of them, she would know how anger would affect the attack, how their customs dictated how they would fight.

This lack of understanding was the only thing that worried her. It was the biggest variable in a very large equation. She could only guess at their reactions. When they had first attacked Earth, they had seemed surprised that humans had retaliated. The successful destruction of some of the alien ships seemed to anger them. Their second attack focused on population centers, though the first hadn't.

It had seemed as if they were retaliating. But Banks knew better than to second-guess the enemy. Perhaps the population centers had always been their chosen targets for the follow-up attack.

She wasn't going to play emotional gambles or emotional bluffs this time. She was fighting an interplanetary war, and she was going to do it by the book. No psychological analysis, no attempts to throw off the enemy. Instead, she was going to fight the best, hardest fight of her life.

And if she had her way, the beautiful ball below her was going to win it.

October 12, 2018
6:30 A.M. Eastern Daylight Time

29 Days Until Second Harvest

Leo Cross's hands were tight on the steering wheel of his car. For the first time in months, he hadn't used the vehicle's automatic navigation system. There were simply too many variables, and he hadn't known how to program them in.

He glanced at the passenger seat. Edwin Bradshaw leaned against the door. He looked pale and nervous. Bradshaw had just turned sixty-one, and even though he took good care of himself, Cross worried about his health. The stresses and strains of the last year had clearly etched themselves on Bradshaw's face. The last of his hair had gone gray and the webbing of fine lines around his eyes had grown deeper.

Cross was almost two decades younger, but he felt

the changes in his own body. A man couldn't survive on adrenaline and four hours of sleep a night forever—not at his age, and certainly not at Bradshaw's. That was a game for younger men. But it was something that Cross no longer had a choice about.

He eased the car over the speed bumps in the parking lot on the Johns Hopkins campus. The buildings in front of him looked like normal university buildings, but inside one hid the main lab for the Space Telescope Science Institute. He pulled into a reserved parking space and put the car in park.

"Beep Britt, will you?" he asked.

Bradshaw nodded as Cross got out of the car. The fall air was warm and smelled faintly of smoke. Not the kind of smoke he used to smell as a kid—that nice, fall smell of burning leaves—but something darker and more ominous, something he didn't really want to identify.

He went to the main doors as Brittany Archer came out.

She was thin—too thin now—and tall. Her dark hair was pulled back in a ponytail, and she wore no makeup. Her clothing was baggy. Her shirt fell off her shoulder, revealing one of the five tattoos she had gotten as a teenager and now regretted. She simply hadn't had the time, or so she claimed, to have them removed.

She was the head of the Institute and a member of the Tenth Planet Project, just like he was. She was also his lover. Their relationship was one of the few good things to have come out of the last year.

She smiled when she saw him and he felt himself

17

smile back. No matter what happened, Britt could always draw a smile from him.

"How bad are the roads?" she asked.

"I shut off the autopilot," Cross said.

She grimaced at him. She had reprogrammed his car's autopilot just last month when she had gotten frustrated with his driving. "I could fix it for you."

He shook his head. "We don't have time."

"I can do it as we drive."

"Britt," he said softly, "don't you know what's going on out here?"

She had come up beside him and he caught a whiff of shampoo and coffee. "I heard about the riots."

She sounded almost defensive. That meant she heard about them, but hadn't paid much attention to the news. He understood: she had been using the telescopes to monitor the tenth planet. She'd been dealing up close and personal with the very cause of the riots—the launching of the alien ships.

"The riots are bad, aren't they?" she said into his silence.

He shrugged. "They're pretty isolated. The problem is that they're unpredictable. An area is stable one minute and the next some kids or idiots or someone comes in and start looting stores. Edwin and I were forced onto several back roads to get here. That's why it took longer than I expected."

She blinked, then looked away, and he realized that she had even been too preoccupied to notice that he was late.

He took her into his arms and pulled her close. Her

body felt frailer than it had even six months ago. This work was eating her from the inside. If he had been surviving on four hours sleep, she'd been surviving on two.

"I wish we could take one day," he whispered into her hair.

She leaned into him. "I wish we didn't have to think about the aliens at all. I wish we were back to the way we were two years ago, when I had to write proposals explaining to Congress why continuing to fund the telescopes was important."

He put his finger under her chin and raised her head so that he could look into her tired eyes. Then he smoothed his hands over her cheeks and kissed her.

"A promise," he said. "For the future."

She smiled. "You're such an optimist, Dr. Cross."

"That's why you're with me," he said, and he wasn't joking.

He knew that they all—the entire human race—had to survive this, because he couldn't allow himself to think of the alternative. He was an archaeologist by training. He had delved into all of human history, had literally touched it with his hands. He knew how deep it went, how old the species was, how inventive and miraculous human culture could be.

He didn't want it to end. Not in thirty days. Not in thirty million days. Not ever.

"I thought we were late," Britt said.

"We are." He let her go. She stepped away from him and the loss of her warmth made him feel odd. Maybe the back of his brain was counting the seconds left after all. Maybe deep down inside he knew that the world was in its final innings.

While he was waiting for them, Bradshaw had climbed into the back of the car. Cross smiled. It was just the kind of nice gesture that Bradshaw usually made.

When his initial tasks on the Tenth Planet Project had been completed, Bradshaw had taken it on himself to become the volunteer grandfather of Portia Groopman, the nanotechnology whiz kid who, Cross hoped, would help with the next battle against the aliens. Bradshaw made sure that she ate regularly, and he actually goaded her into an occasional night's sleep. He threatened to rent her an apartment when all of this was over—even though, Cross knew, Portia Groopman was worth enough that she could buy a city block.

Bradshaw believed that there was still time for the niceties of life. Perhaps it was his perspective as the older member of the team. Perhaps it had always been his way. Or perhaps he had learned it during the years when all of his work had been discredited, before Cross proved that Bradshaw had built the foundation for the discoveries that Cross eventually made. Discoveries that led to the discovery of the tenth planet.

Now Bradshaw was supervising a group of graduate students who were delving into the archaeological record to see if there was a time when the tenth planet hadn't come to Earth.

Cross had discovered the tenth planet using the combined fields of archaeology and astronomy—essentially using the record buried in the Earth to learn the history of the universe. He had found a "soot layer" that repeated every 2006 years, and in trying to understand it, had realized that it had come from space. That soot layer, which he had now seen in real time in California, had been the first and best sign of a long history of repeated occurrences.

The tenth planet had an elliptical 2006-year orbit around the Sun. For all but a year of that orbit, the planet was in the cold and dark. Life did not form in such conditions, and Cross and the other scientists speculated that once upon a time, the tenth planet revolved around a different sun, in a more standard, Earth-like orbit.

Something had changed, had brought the tenth planet to this sun and led the inhabitants of that planet to use Earth as its food source. They visited Earth twice each orbit, first as their planet passed Earth's orbit on the way in toward the sun, then again as it passed Earth's orbit on the way out into the cold of deep space. Each time the aliens dropped nanomachines on areas of the Earth to harvest organic material. The nanomachines left behind a black ash that eventually compressed into the soot layer.

The aliens never denuded Earth—they apparently understood the need to keep things growing—but they had never been attacked before either. Cross had gotten the idea that the archaeological record might carry more information than he thought, so he'd assigned Bradshaw some of the best archaeological minds on the university level and sent them out to study the past again.

The point was to see when the tenth planet had first arrived in this solar system. Cross wasn't sure yet what that information would gain him, but he had learned a long time ago that his hunches were worth following.

Britt climbed in the passenger seat, Cross in the driver's seat. He put the car in reverse and backed out. Britt braced herself with a hand on the dash. Her knuckles were white and he wasn't even out of the parking lot yet.

"I could reprogram the autopilot," she said again. "While you're driving."

Cross wasn't going to argue with her—and he wasn't going to let her touch the navigation system while the car was in motion. They still had a lot of driving to do, and he knew that the unrest would get worse the closer they got to downtown Washington.

Ever since some nut had blown up the main entry to the Capitol, that building, with its blackened center, had become a rallying point for other crazies. The rioting had been worse there.

The meeting for the Tenth Planet Project had been moved from its location near the Capitol, but they hadn't gone too far. Most of the major members of the Project worked in that area, and these days they didn't have time to travel large distances.

Britt let go of the dash and let her right hand hover over the navigation system. Cross took her fingers in his own. "We have more important things to worry about," he said.

"Leo—"

"How many ships launched, Britt?" he asked. She

probably thought he wanted to distract her, but he didn't. He hadn't had a chance to talk to her, really talk to her, in days. He didn't want to get all of the news at the meeting. He wanted to be able to discuss some of it with her. "The news never said."

"On purpose." She slid her hand from his then eased his fingers back on the steering wheel. She was younger than he was, just enough to trust a computer's driving skills over a person's. He, on the other hand, never completely trusted a computer and could never quite overlook the glitches they used to cause.

"People are already rioting," Bradshaw said from the backseat. "How much worse could the news be?"

Britt turned toward him, the look on her face both weary and old. With Bradshaw's question, she had clearly forgotten the driving debate; somehow that alarmed Cross more than her initial response had.

"Britt?" Cross asked again. "How many ships left the tenth planet?"

"A hundred and eight." Her words were soft. Cross felt the hair rise on the back of his neck. The aliens were using a few more ships than they had used the last time they had attacked Earth. Then they had sent one hundred one. The coming attack would be at least as bad as the first one. And that one had left whole chunks of the planet devastated.

"I don't understand," Bradshaw said. "People know ships are coming toward Earth. Why not tell them how many?"

"It's not my decision." Britt turned around and slumped on the passenger side.

The car was entering a new neighborhood, and as it did, Cross saw a gang of men setting fire to a building at the end of the block. He looked away. He certainly couldn't get out of the car and help. In fact, all news outlets had been warning people to stay away from the rioting area.

"Britt," he said, "use your phone to report a disturbance down here."

She glanced at him, then used her wrist'puter to dial the emergency number. The computerized dispatch took the information but did not promise a response time. The police and emergency response units were already stressed to the breaking point. Cross and Bradshaw had called other disturbances in and had received the same responses.

Finally, Britt shut off her link and ran a hand through her hair. She sighed. "What about you guys?"

"What about us?" Cross saw smoke near the Beltway. He sighed. They'd have to take more back routes.

"What have you found?"

He knew the tactic. Britt didn't want to talk about the ships anymore.

"We know more about these aliens than I ever thought possible," Bradshaw said.

Cross nodded. "We're going to lay out most of this at the meeting. We've put a lot together in the last few weeks."

He was amazed at how little he had been able to share with her lately. When they got together, they often ate a late meal and fell asleep in each other's arms, too tired for anything else.

They had to save the world, he thought wryly, just so that he could have a day off with Britt.

"Fill me in," Britt said. "I hate surprises at meetings."

The street ahead was blocked with two ruined taxicabs. All of the buildings' windows were broken, and glass covered the concrete. Cross turned down a side street.

"We've learned," he said as if nothing were wrong, "from the doctors working with the bodies recovered from the alien ships we shot down, that the aliens evolved on a stable, warm planet, covered with oceans. They have a methane-rich atmosphere, and a gravity about one tenth lighter than ours."

"We know from using a special dating of material from their ships," Bradshaw said, "that the material has been frozen and thawed at least six thousand times. And the aliens themselves show signs of slight cell damage caused by repeated freezing and thawing."

"Six thousand?" Britt asked, turning to stare at Bradshaw, clearly shocked.

"Amazing, isn't it?" Cross asked. "It seems they have developed a way to hibernate for all but a year of the two thousand and six years of their planet's orbit. Then when their planet comes in close to the sun, they revive, harvest supplies from our planet, and go back into cold sleep for another two thousand years."

"But six thousand times?" Britt asked. "How is that possible?"

"We don't know," Cross said. "That number matches what Edwin's archaeological grad student group has come up with in Earth records, and orbital changes caused by the arrival of the tenth planet into the system. We know for certain that the tenth planet came from outside our system, and the aliens have been visiting Earth every two thousand and six years for the last twelve million years."

"Twelve million years?" Britt said. "Wow."

"We must have been a real surprise to them when they thawed out this time," Bradshaw said.

Cross grinned. He hadn't thought about it that way before. After thousands of years of fairly primitive response, humans had finally come into their own.

Humans finally had the ability to defend themselves—not just on the ground, but in space.

"Let's just hope," Britt said, "we have enough to surprise them one more time."

Cross glanced at her. Her wan features seemed determined.

"I think we can," he said, as much to reassure her as himself.

2

October 12, 2018
14:37 Universal Time

29 Days Until Second Harvest

Cicoi, Commander of the South, stood at his command post, his upper tentacles resting on the controls, his lower tentacles wrapped around the command circle, and his eyestalks extended. The warship glided smoothly beneath him, heading toward the third planet.

The visuals were on, so that the walls seemed to have disappeared. Instead it looked as if he and his staff were floating, unprotected, through the vastness of space.

Ahead of them was the third planet, its ugly blue-and-white mass looming in his imagination. He wondered what surprises it would bring this time. He knew that it was his job to make certain that the surprises did not hurt Malmur.

Unlike the last time he took out this warship, this

time he was prepared for any contingency. His staff was well trained and used to the unusual configuration. They were scattered throughout the large command center. They stood on circles that extended from the walls according to rank. If he looked down, he could see them, seemingly unsupported, against the darkness of universe.

Round balls, representing information feeds from the third planet, floated before most of his staff. The energy use still astonished and worried Cicoi. All of it was precious and all of it could be used to survive the next period of darkness. But, he had to remind himself, there might not be another period of darkness if he did not subdue the third planet.

His mission sounded simple: harvest the third planet with no additional loss of life or ships. But Cicoi, who had tried to destroy most of the weapons the third planet had launched at Malmur, knew that the word "simple" no longer applied to the third planet.

If the Malmuria had followed tradition, Cicoi would have been recycled after his failure. He had allowed fifteen of the weapons through the defenses. They had exploded on Malmur's surface, sending odd-shaped clouds into the atmosphere. Strange fires had burned on the ground, and all Malmuria near the explosions had died.

Two pods and all their opening nestlings were gone.

An entire sleeping chamber, filled with thousands of unawakened Malmuria, had been vaporized.

Eight harvest ships were destroyed. Huge areas of

the vast energy collectors that surrounded the planet had been ruined.

And that was only the beginning of the destruction.

The nestlings in three other pods had wasted away and died of some horrible lingering sickness that the Malmuria had never seen before. Long ago, they had eliminated the need for traditional healers, and so they had no one besides the female caregivers to help the nestlings.

Some of the female caregivers had grown ill as well, and several of the older ones had died. Some of the brood females had laid deformed eggs into the pods. There was debate now as to whether or not those eggs should be recycled.

The strange clouds had dissipated into the atmosphere, and the radiation levels on Malmur had risen. No one had known how to fix that. And some of the farseeing males, the ones who specialized in preparing for the future, worried that the Malmuria hadn't seen the results of all of the destruction yet.

All of this because Cicoi and his fleet had allowed fifteen weapons through. He shuddered to think what would have happened had he not stopped any of them. He believed, although he said nothing to anyone, that Malmur itself would have been destroyed.

As his fleet had returned to Malmur, he had planned to offer himself and his crew to the recycler. All failures went to the recycler where they were converted to energy and made into something more useful to their people. But the Elders had stopped him.

The great Commanders of the past had put themselves into the recyclers when they had failed to complete the First Harvest of this Pass. They had lost ships, something that had never happened before, and so they had destroyed themselves, without really training their replacements.

The Elders had argued that if Cicoi and his fellow Commanders did the same, the Malmuria would have no experienced leaders left. Cicoi privately thought that his experience was not the kind that the Malmuria wanted, but he had not argued with the Elders.

When the Elders had been living, breathing creatures, instead of the black spirits they were now, they had saved Malmur from certain destruction. Once, Cicoi knew, the Malmuria had fought among themselves. The Elders had been the ones who had united the planet.

They had found a way to release Malmur from its sun to save the entire race. They had sent Malmur into the depths of interstellar space until it found itself in a new orbit, around this new sun. They had devised the system of harvesting and darkness that had become the new order.

The Elders had roused themselves from the spirit rest to guide Malmur through this new crisis. An Elder flew on this warship. He was not visible at the moment. As Malmur got closer to the third planet and the plans were finalized, he was present less and less. Cicoi worried that the Elder was vanishing not because he had come to trust Cicoi—Cicoi believed the Elder would never completely trust him—but because the Elder's own personal energy, whatever it was, was fading.

Cicoi hoped the Elders could hang on through this battle.

Even though Cicoi had been chosen to be Commander of this entire mission, he answered to the Elders. The Elders were the ones who had come up with the new plan. They were the ones who had insisted that the fleet consist of eighteen warships and ninety harvesters. Cicoi had argued that more harvesters were needed—no harvest had ever been done with as few as ninety ships—but the Elders had been adamant.

They had also insisted that the harvesters return one final time. The Malmuria would do a third harvesting pass, where in the past they had only done two.

All of this change made Cicoi's tentacles flake. Never before, not in all of the Passes he'd lived through, had tradition been so thoroughly violated.

His Elder dismissed tradition, saying it had stifled growth on Malmur. Cicoi knew that sometimes the Elder did not understand how life worked now on Malmur. Gone were the days of continual sunshine and warmth and abundant energy. Gone was the luxury of time. From the moment the Malmuria woke from their long sleep, they were struggling to raise nestlings, fill pods, and provide enough food and energy to make it through the long darkness.

Never before had Cicoi seen his people suffer such

defeats. Never before had he seen them respond with such passion and anger. He hadn't believed that they would be able to make the eighteen warships functional in time, nor had he believed that the staff of those ships could be trained in this new method of flight, but it had happened.

It had happened, but it had cost a lot of energy. It had prevented thousands of sleepers from waking, and he knew that the brood females—the ones who were still healthy—would not be able to raise sufficient nestlings next pass.

Cicoi felt his eyestalks quiver every time he thought about the destroyed young lives.

The future of his people hung in the balance. It was up to him to save them. If he did, he would redeem himself.

There would still be hardship, of course. More hardship than they had ever experienced. But his people were more unified than they had been since the days of the Elders. And now his people knew they could accomplish more during their period of wakefulness than they had ever done in the past. That would help.

If everything went smoothly.

Three Passes instead of two meant everything had to go perfectly.

Cicoi turned his eyestalks toward the image of the third planet. Nothing had gone perfectly during this awakening. But he couldn't let that defeat him, or he would lose everything.

Malmur had to survive.

October 12, 2018
7:50 A.M. Eastern Daylight Time

29 Days Until Second Harvest

This conference room was as different from the original one as a conference room could be. The old conference room had had a cramped 1980s design. This one was modern, with shaded glass walls and a feeling of space, even though it was three levels underground.

Leo Cross had a feeling that this conference room was one he normally would have never seen. The building was unmarked, like the previous building, and a woman in black wearing a security tag had met them at the door. Then he, Britt, and Bradshaw had gone through an elaborate security process that included passing through a high-level scanner and some lasers, as well as the latest airport screening equipment.

The woman had also had them all place their hands on a print scanner, and a cool sexless digitized voice had identified them. That procedure itself took almost fifteen minutes. When it was completed, a different woman, also wearing black, met them on the other side of the security barrier. She was the one who led them through a series of corridors to an elevator that dropped them three levels in the space of a heartbeat. The elevator opened onto the conference room. They saw nothing else of the building.

Cross knew that spread out below the entire city

were tunnels and secure facilities designed for the president, members of Congress, and other top government officials so that they could keep the government operating during an attack on D.C. As a boy, he had toured the old underground facilities—the ones that had been built during the Cold War—with his parents. The government still acted as if that old series of tunnels was all that remained of such lavish and outdated fears.

But Cross's friend, Doug Mickelson, had once commented that the government would be stupid not to plan for any contingency. This building, with its elaborate security procedures and its ultramodern design, made it clear to Cross that the paranoia of those first underground security tunnels had never gone away.

He only hoped that this place was sturdy enough to withstand attack from the aliens' nanomachines. It wasn't new enough to have been designed and built after the first alien attack.

This building was a good mile away from the last one. It was also farther away from the traditional seats of power, but he had a feeling that General Maddox had chosen this place for reasons besides that. It would be easy for her to get to—she had even less time than the rest of them—and it probably had satellite hookups built into those glass walls.

"Yuck," Britt said as the elevator doors closed, and the elevator left, taking their guide with it. "No windows."

Bradshaw looked at her with surprise. "You don't have windows in your lab."

She grinned at him. "Who needs windows there when you can see the entire universe?"

"She's got you there," Cross said. He stepped deeper into the room. The air was climate controlled to a somewhat cool sixty-eight degrees. It smelled recycled, so he bet it was on its own system. Someone had laid out fresh pastries, and several kinds of coffee rested on a table against the far wall.

There were small groupings of furniture, easy chairs mixed with end tables, in case people wanted to split up and have private discussions. But the rest of the conference room was dominated by the table.

Cross walked over to it and ran his fingers across it. The surface was the same shaded glass that covered the walls. The chairs surrounding it were large, comfortable, and expensive. They were also the kind that, without prompting from their occupant, fitted themselves to the occupant's body shape.

And to think Cross had been worried about this neighborhood when he had driven into it. Some of the rioting was less than a block away. As he had turned into the parking garage, a military squadron had run past, bodies moving in unison, weapons clutched in the ready position.

He hadn't realized until he came down here that the presence of troops here had probably been very necessary. At least his car—which had gone through several security beams on its way to the assigned parking spot—would be safe.

As was he. He was probably safer here than he had ever been in his life.

"What is this place?" Britt asked.

"It's probably better not to ask." Bradshaw glanced at Cross, who nodded once. Bradshaw got the same sense of this place that Cross had.

The elevator doors purred open and three more people got out. Robert Shane, who headed the president's Special Committee on Space Sciences, walked directly toward the pastries. He had clearly been here before. He was one of the cooler heads on the Project, and Cross had been relieved to have him at the meetings more than once.

"Mmmm," Shane said as he picked up a heavily frosted cinnamon roll. "Still warm."

This time Britt looked startled. No bakeries were open—no stores were open, not since the rioting had begun. The entire city was under martial law, like cities all over the world, and when the disturbances began, sensible people stopped going to their day jobs. That was why the streets had been mostly empty of other drivers, other cars. The only people outside right now were the looters and rioters, and people with a mission, like the members of the Tenth Planet Project.

Yolanda Hayes, the president's science adviser, examined the room the same way Cross had. Her dark eyes took in the glass, the modern furniture, the specialized table.

Jesse Killius, the head of NASA, did the same.

Cross looked at Shane again. If the women had never seen this room before, and they outranked Shane, then he had seen it for some other project.

Long ago, Cross had learned that Shane had a high

ranking in the Air Force. Perhaps he had seen this place in connection with his military work, not his relationship with the president.

For some reason that thought sent shivers through Cross.

"They are warm!" Britt said.

Cross turned. She was standing beside Shane, a blueberry muffin in hand.

"How'd they manage that?" she asked.

"Probably baked special for us," Shane said, grabbing a paper plate. "And I, for one, am not going to let them go to waste."

Baked special on the premises somewhere. Cross walked to the pastry table, saw some petit fours, which he usually despised, as well as cookies of all shapes and sizes, the huge cinnamon rolls—frosting melting off of them—and the muffins.

He grabbed a muffin and poured himself some of the regular coffee that someone had already brewed. Britt had wandered over to the major coffee-making equipment and was surveying it. When she had her choice, he knew she always made a cappuccino.

Yolanda Hayes ran her fingers across the glass table just like Cross had done. Then she sat in a chair on the left center, and squeaked, looking down at her seat.

"This chair just grabbed me!" she said.

"They're made to do that," Cross said. "Very expensive. You're supposed to be more comfortable now."

"I don't know." Hayes's dark skin had flushed rose. "I'm thinking that I may sue this chair for sexual harassment."

"Enjoy it," Killius said as she walked to the pastry table. "These days, we're all so busy we should take what we can get."

Shane let out a bark of a laugh and then clamped his mouth closed, as if his own reaction had startled him. He took the chair across from Hayes and grinned at her. "I'm with Jesse on this one."

"Yeah, well, I'm rethinking," Hayes said. "This chair may be fresh, but it only has one move."

"That you know of," Britt said as the cappuccino maker made a whooshing noise.

Cross's hand hovered over the cookies. It seemed indelicate somehow to be looking at fresh-baked pastries and elaborate chairs as the world was falling apart around them. The thought, instead of dampening his interest in the food, seemed to heighten it. Survival reaction, he told himself, and grabbed a chocolate chip cookie to go with his coffee and muffin.

He put his food down beside Hayes, leaving the chair closest to the head of the table for Britt. His chair shifted beneath him, and then provided padding where he needed it, lengthened to fit his legs, and put a support against his back.

Even though he was prepared for it, the experience was still a bit disconcerting.

Bradshaw sat down on the other side of Shane. He had only poured himself a glass of water. He seemed more nervous than usual.

Bradshaw wasn't an official member of the Tenth Planet Project, although he had attended meetings before. He was here this time because he had done a lot more of the basic research into the aliens than Cross had. Also, since the announcement of the alien ships, Cross wanted company whenever he got in his car. Bradshaw probably wouldn't leap to anyone's rescue—he was too smart to get involved in brawls—but he would contact emergency services fast.

As if they would be able to respond in this mess.

The elevator doors opened again and Portia Groopman stood beside the security guard. Portia was wearing a dress for the first time since Cross had met her, and her hair was combed away from her face. She had put lipstick on, but had chewed through the layer on her lower lip. In her right hand, she clutched one of her stuffed dogs.

If he hadn't known she was one of the most talented nanotechnology researchers in the world, he would have thought she was someone's daughter who had gotten lost in the building. She was only nineteen and had been homeless many of those years. As a result, she was even quirkier than most scientists he had met.

"I didn't know you were coming, Portia," Cross said, glancing at Bradshaw. He hadn't moved either. "I could have given you a ride."

"I wish you had," Portia said. "I didn't know the streets were so bad. I had to keep hitting reset on my car's navigator."

"I thought I'd tell them about the research," Bradshaw said.

"That was the plan," Portia said. "Then I got to thinking about it. I want everyone to understand exactly what we're doing. Can I explain it now?"

She hadn't even gotten off the elevator. The security guard looked nervously around the room.

"Not everyone's here yet," Britt said. "Come on in and have some pastries."

"Pastries?" Portia stepped off the elevator. The security guard looked relieved as the doors closed and took her away from the meeting. "You guys are gorging while people are looting grocery stores?"

Shane put down his cinnamon roll. "I guess you could look at it that way," he said. "Or you could say that, unlike the people on the street, we assume that civilization is going to continue."

"My stomach likes your philosophy better," Portia said. She walked to the table, keeping the stuffed dog tight against her ribs.

"How'd she get in?" Cross asked Bradshaw softly.

"Maddox gave her security clearance two meetings ago," Bradshaw said. "She just preferred to send me. I think she's here this time because she's nervous."

"I am not," Portia said, but the way she held that dog belied her words. "I just want to make sure everyone understands what's going on."

A door on the side of the glass wall hissed open, and General Clarissa Maddox entered. Through the door, Cross caught a glimpse of a wide corridor, and several military personnel. Then the view vanished.

Portia hurried to one of the few remaining chairs

and set the dog on the table beside the pile of cookies she had taken.

Bradshaw raised an eyebrow at Cross, a silent signal that Maddox's arrival confirmed his suspicions.

"Thank you all for coming," Maddox said as she took her position at the head of the table. "Britt, would you mind grabbing me a cinnamon roll? I haven't eaten yet this morning."

Things had changed in the last six months. Early in their relationship, Britt would have bristled at the order, but now she did it without complaint.

"Let's get started," Maddox said. "I don't have a lot of time here, and I suspect none of the rest of you do either."

Then she paused and frowned at Portia.

"I'm Portia Groopman." Portia's voice shook. "From NanTech? You said you wanted to hear about my research. I know that was a while back, but—"

"I know who you are," Maddox said. "I don't understand the purpose of the stuffed dog. If it's for demonstration, then place it beside you until you need it."

Cross opened his mouth to explain that Portia usually had a stuffed animal with her, but before he could say anything, Portia had hidden the dog under the table.

"All right," Maddox said. "Let's get underway."

Britt set the roll in front of Maddox along with some regular coffee, then slipped into her chair. Maddox ran her finger along the edge of the table, and as she did, the walls sprang to life. Tiny screens appeared and on them, the rest of advisers to the Tenth Planet Project.

Representatives from every major country in the world appeared on the screens, as well as science advisers and specialists. Most of them were sitting at old-fashioned conference tables, although a few of the Middle Eastern countries seemed to provide only chairs.

The effect was eerie: dozens of screens against the blackness of the wall. Britt ran a hand along the tabletop, where the screens were reflected.

"Thank you all for coming," Maddox said. "We have a lot of ground to cover, so let's limit any discussion to important questions and clarifications. Any details can be dealt with later."

Cross pushed his plate away. He suddenly found himself not interested in the food.

"I understand from the vid reports and the updates we're getting here that the rioting we're experiencing in the United States has spread worldwide," Maddox said.

Several leaders from several of the countries started to speak at once. Maddox held up her hand for silence. It surprised Cross that they had spoken up so soon after she had warned them not to, but it didn't seem to surprise Maddox.

"If you remember, we expected some unrest when it became clear that we hadn't destroyed the aliens. The key now," Maddox said, "is to contain it."

"These are national concerns," said Maddox's Japanese counterpart.

"No, they're not," Maddox said. "Right now, we face a threat to our entire planet. If we can't respond as a unified force, we may as well kiss our respective asses good-bye."

Cross wrapped his fingers around his coffee mug, grateful for the warmth. Britt was looking down. She really didn't seem to want to deal with the unrest at all.

"The diplomats have already resolved the jurisdiction issue," Maddox was saying. "I'm just here to inform you all of the plan."

Cross straightened. He hadn't expected a plan on this issue to be addressed here.

"The president of the United States will speak to the world tonight," Maddox said. "He will explain the preparations we have made to fight the aliens. He will tell the average citizen what to do and where it will be safe for them to go. He will lay the fears that are causing this rioting to rest."

"Pardon me, General," said the British representative, "but there is no way your president will actually reach the rioters. Those people will be on the streets destroying property while he attempts to address them."

"As I said," Maddox's fingers ripped at the cinnamon roll. It looked like a nervous movement to Cross. "The diplomats have already worked this out. It's my understanding that the president's speech will reach several billion viewers, and the idea is that those viewers will then spread the word to the people on the street."

"We certainly can't expect the military to continue to quell the unrest," Shane said. He was looking directly at Maddox, but Cross knew that Shane was speaking for the benefit of the other countries. "We need our forces to concentrate on the alien threat."

"I think the main problem here isn't the deployment of the military," Maddox said, "but the fact that we want as much of the infrastructure to remain. Right now, people lack a plan, so they are reacting—some are cowering, others are acting out. Once they know what they can do, the theory is that they will do it."

She didn't sound convinced. Cross thought the idea had merit, though. The quicker this unrest died down, the better for all of them.

"Ms. Groopman," Maddox said. "Since you're our guest, update us on your nanotechnology work."

"Before she does," Cross said, "let me explain to our allies that Portia has been the person in charge of our nanotechnology research from the beginning."

He didn't mention that some of the nanotechnology research had been funneled to the U.S. government and was now top secret. He figured that Maddox didn't want the other governments to know that.

He went on. "Portia's the one who identified the fossils Dr. Bradshaw found as some form of nanomachine and she's the one who correctly discovered their purpose. She's been working with the live nanoharvesters that we recovered from the Monterey site."

And getting no sleep doing it, he knew. She had worked harder than any of them, and she had made some tremendous breakthroughs.

"Do I have to stand?" Portia asked softly.

"No, honey," Jesse Killius said. "But you will have to speak up."

Color stained Portia's cheeks. She reached for the dog, then seemed to think better of it.

44

"You told them about the nanorescuers, right?" she asked Cross.

He nodded. Nanorescuer was the name of the nanomachines that Portia had designed to neutralize the aliens' nanoharvesters. The harvesters were pernicious little things, smaller than a speck of dust, that dissolved and stored organic material. They didn't move, fortunately, but they did "eat" until there was no organic material left near them.

Initially Portia and her team had tried to find a way to shut off the nanoharvesters, but she had been unsuccessful. Cross believed the government scientists were still working on just that and hadn't found one either. So one day she had gotten an idea that she could create a nanomachine that would attack the harvesters. Cross told her to follow up on it, without consulting the Tenth Planet Project, thinking that there was no point in duplicating the other research—she was better doing research on her own.

Portia created the nanorescuers, which were drawn to the nanoharvesters like magnets were drawn to metal. Once they touched the harvesters, they sucked all the energy from the alien machines, rendering them useless.

Cross had informed the Project of her discovery weeks ago. Since then, Bradshaw had kept them up to date. This was Portia's first appearance before the group. He wondered why she thought today important enough to come herself.

"Um." Portia glanced at Maddox, then at the screens on the walls. "We have twenty different facilities working around the clock to make nanorescuers. These facilities are at full production. NanTech has devoted all of its resources to this, and so have other U.S. nanotech companies."

Maddox folded her hands on the table. The gesture seemed to calm Portia. Bradshaw was nodding his encouragement.

Cross just watched her, knowing that almost anything could throw her off her rhythm.

"By the end of the week, a hundred plants, government and private, will be making the nanorescuers. It looks like, by the week before the aliens arrive, another thousand factories around the world will be on mass production schedules."

"Thank you, Ms. Groopman," Maddox said. Portia bit her lower lip as if she'd been chastised. "Now—"

"Wait," Cross said. "Portia hasn't come to see us before, and I know she could have had me or Edwin give that report. There's something else, isn't there, Portia?"

Portia's glance darted nervously around the table. "Yeah," she said as softly as she had before. This time, she grabbed her dog and clung to it like it was a lifeline. "We could use more factories to make the nanorescuers. And we're going to need some more specialists to oversee production and to train people. NanTech doesn't have the resources to do much more than we're doing, and building the prototypes as we bring new factories on-line is exacting work."

Maddox gave the dog a sharp glance, but wisely said nothing. Cross wondered if anyone else even noticed it.

"What do you suggest?" Maddox asked.

"We'll train specialists at NanTech if they can arrive this week," Portia said. "We want to do the training all at once. That prevents us from diverting our own resources."

Maddox nodded. "We'll handle the details of this after the formal meeting. What else?"

Portia licked her lips. "We have no idea how many nanoharvesters the aliens are going to release. I'm planning for worst case. We don't want to be caught by surprise."

"Agreed," Maddox said, but her tone was measured.

"I want to have enough rescuers to blanket the world twice over," Portia said. "Right now we're barely going to make once over, and I'm afraid we'll miss areas."

"I think we will miss many areas," Maddox said. "The other problem is delivery of the nanorescuers."

"We talked about dusting the Earth with them. I mean, didn't you?" Portia was looking at Cross now. "That's what I understood—"

"Yes," Cross said. "I told them. That's what we plan."

"The problem," Shane said, "is with delivery. I've been put in charge of coordinating this section of the Project."

Cross knew that was because of his position with the Air Force, but Portia obviously didn't know who Shane was. She was staring at him as if she were trying to figure that out.

Shane turned toward Maddox, as if to get approval to give his part of the report now. She nodded almost imperceptibly. Portia pulled the dog tighter and leaned back in her chair.

"Every small working plane in every country is being impounded and fitted for crop dusting of the nanorescuers," Shane said. "We've also drafted every person who can fly small planes—or at least everyone we can find. Most of the countries have a standing request out for volunteers."

Some countries had made no requests, Cross knew. Some had ordered compliance. Shane was tactfully skipping over the different methods of the varied sovereignties. Everyone had been skipping over those things. Right now, as someone had pointed out earlier, the most important thing was for the world to work together, not to fight over differences in methodology.

"We hope to be able to blanket the world, as Ms. Groopman said," Shane continued, "but the way it looks—based solely on delivery methods—we'll only be able to dust cities and towns."

"But what about the people who live in villages or the country?" Britt asked. She sounded shocked.

"That's part of the president's speech tonight," Maddox said. "He's going to tell people to move to populated areas for safety reasons."

"So the cities are going to be overrun," Cross muttered.

Britt elbowed him.

But that didn't stop him. "General," he said, "people can go to deserts as well. The aliens aren't going to touch areas that aren't lush. I think we should also launch as many ships as possible, oceans only, of course. That should take some of the pressure off the cities."

"Good point," Maddox said. "I will make sure that gets mentioned as well."

"That still won't take all the stress off the cities," Bradshaw said.

"We have a month to make this transition," Shane said. "It's not like people have to be to a major city tomorrow. In fact, the dusting won't even start until two days before the aliens' arrival, and it will continue throughout the attack."

Portia was shaking her head. "Two flybys should be enough," she said. "Let's spread the rescuers other places. I mean, these aliens are going for crops, too. If they destroy the unpopulated areas, how are we going to feed people?"

Her words echoed in the large room.

"We have to make it through the attack first," Maddox said. "Then we worry about the aftermath."

Portia leaned forward. "But if we do it my way—"

"Ms. Groopman, the issue has already been decided."

"But we can't. We have to spread them all over—"

"Portia," Cross said quietly. "No one here made the decision. It came from upstairs and is already being implemented."

"Idiots," Portia mumbled. "They should have consulted with me."

They had seen her recommendations, Cross knew. He also knew that the world leaders were trying to solve two problems here: they wanted people to survive the alien attack and they wanted to stop the unrest.

Then Cross glanced at Maddox. She seemed to be working to suppress a smile. Apparently, she had agreed with Portia.

"I think Ms. Groopman has a point," Maddox said. "Let's make sure that when we report to our superiors we mention the possible future food shortages. I'm sure FEMA and the equivalent organizations in other countries have already thought of making sure enough food is in the cities to feed the added population. But we should also be stockpiling seeds—things will grow in that ash, won't they?"

Cross nodded. "If the aliens do as they have in the past," he said. "We discovered soot layers buried under centuries of organic material. They don't permanently harm the Earth, but I'm not a biologist. I can't guarantee whether we'll have a growing season at all after the nanoharvesters land."

"Forgive me for interrupting," said one of the members of the Argentinean team. "We have already seen plants begin to recover in the rainforests."

"Good," Maddox said. "Then the next growing season will go on as usual."

"But that doesn't make up for all the lost food," Portia said.

"We're getting off track," Maddox said firmly. "This work is very important, and if I had the power to alter the commands of the world leaders, I would do so. But right now, we are dusting only major population centers, and we will make sure people are in those centers.

Dr. Shane, if you or someone can guarantee us a better delivery method, I might be able to bring an altered plan to the president. Otherwise, this plan remains."

Cross felt a shiver run down his back. It was a minimal damage plan. People would die in the country and villages. Some of them would just refuse to leave. He hoped that his assessment was right; that the aliens would continue to target fertile areas only.

Portia looked down. She obviously didn't like this plan at all. Perhaps she was still young enough to believe they would all survive this. Or perhaps she was in denial about the extent of the problem that faced them.

Maybe, with all the work she'd been doing, she hadn't even had time to think about it. Cross decided that he'd try to talk with her later. He didn't want her angry at the program so that she stopped working hard. She was one of their very best assets.

"Anything new on the ships?" Maddox asked Britt.

"We haven't been able to observe much yet," she said. "At the moment, we estimate that there are one hundred and eight ships coming our way."

This sparked discussion among all the groups— worry that this was just the first wave of ships, and concern that the ships would use more nanoharvesters than before. Some worried that the aliens were going to use new, different weapons on the Earth.

Maddox agreed that all of this was possible, but that there was no evidence to support any of it.

While the discussion continued, Cross watched Portia. She had left her cookie stack alone. She was cuddling the stuffed dog and plucking at its fur. The conversation about the nanorescuers had bothered her. She obviously wanted to blanket the entire planet, and she was disturbed at the changes in the plan.

After a moment, Bradshaw entered the discussion, explaining what his grad student group had discovered about the aliens. Some of the biologists talked about their studies of the dead aliens, and what the theories were.

Cross forced himself to look away from Portia and concentrate on the conversation. He knew all of this stuff, so it wasn't of much interest to him, and he knew that Bradshaw could handle much of it on his own.

It wasn't until one of the Egyptians said, "I do not care whether the aliens need our planet as a food source. I do not believe that understanding the enemy makes much difference in this case."

Cross stared at the man on the screen. He looked fierce. Maddox started to answer, but Cross said softly, "Let me."

Maddox nodded.

Cross said, "We don't know a lot about these aliens. We don't know their cultural norms. We don't know how they are born, how they raise their young, or how they live when they're not at war. What we do know is that they are intelligent, they are—or were for many millennia—significantly more advanced than we are, and that they work well together in groups."

The Egyptian was watching, arms crossed. Some of the other scientists leaned forward. Cross felt a shiver run through him. Britt had told him time and time again that people listened to him more than they listened to the others. It surprised him every time he saw evidence of it.

"The biggest thing that we know is that they harvest Earth like lost travelers in the desert would harvest an oasis. As far as we can tell, we are their only food source. For thousands upon thousands of years, we did not fight back."

His voice was rising. He tried to keep it in check. He didn't want to sound strident, even though he was feeling that way.

"It would be as if every animal group that we slaughtered for food, from chickens to cows, suddenly started fighting back—and also fighting to protect the crops and the grass around them. That's what I believe these aliens are facing."

"So?" the Egyptian said. "I cannot—I will not—feel compassion for them."

Cross let out a small breath. Ah, that was where this argument was going, then. "When we try to understand the aliens, we're not doing it so that we can empathize with them. We're not doing it so that we feel compassion. We're doing it to try to second-guess how they will attack us."

Maddox folded her hands together. Portia was watching him over the head of the small dog. Britt was squeezing her cappuccino cup so hard her knuckles were white.

"I believe, and this is just my belief, that these aliens believe this is a fight to the death." Cross glanced at the other screens. Heads were nodding at tables all over the world. "I think they are fighting for their own survival and we're fighting for ours. They're not going to come in, retaliate, and leave. They have to harvest food from this planet, or their species will die. That means that they'll have to defeat us, at least by their game plan. I think this next fight will be extremely difficult."

The Egyptian bowed his head once. "If you put it that way," he said, "I will agree with you. I would like to hear less psychoanalysis, however, and more about ways that we can *physically* defeat them."

"Well," Maddox said before Cross could speak again, "let me tell you what I can of the military plans."

What she could? Cross glanced at her. She was a smart woman, one of the members of the Joint Chiefs of Staff. She chose her words with great care. Obviously, she felt she couldn't share all of the plans. And now he was wondering why. But he knew better than to challenge her in front of their international peers.

"We have come up with a method of attacking the alien ships," Maddox said.

Cross held his breath. No one had told him this and, judging from the surprised looks around the table, no one had told anyone on the U.S. part of the Tenth Planet Project.

"Why didn't you tell us this before?" Yolanda Hayes asked.

"I wasn't at liberty to," Maddox said. She smiled. Apparently the silence hadn't bothered her. "Let me explain what we're going to do."

Her smile grew and she rubbed her hands together. Obviously this part of the plan pleased her. "All of you remember the first attack. Nothing electronic can get through the aliens' dampening fields. They have some kind of equipment that steals the energy from anything within a certain radius."

Most of that, Cross knew, was for the members who hadn't been in the Project during the first attack. The aliens' dampening fields had been part of the problem from the very beginning and the subject of many meetings.

"We have figured out a way around this. We are going to have planes fly *above* the dampening fields. As the alien ships approach the ground so that they can release the nanoharvesters, we will drop bombs on the ships from above."

Maddox had all of their attention now. Cross's stomach was in knots and he didn't quite know why.

"Government scientists who have been working on parts of the alien ships have found a material that will stick to the hulls. We are going to use bombs that will stick and do no immediate harm. Instead of having an electrical timer, these bombs will have a simple altitude pressure switch that requires no electronics at all. When the alien ships rise to a certain altitude, the switch will trigger and the bombs will blow. We believe that enough bombs, dropped on the ships, will destroy the ships."

"But the harvesters will already have been released," Killius said.

Maddox nodded. She seemed almost annoyed that the first response was a negative one. Cross had to admit he was stunned by the news and was searching, in his own mind, to find a hole in the idea. Because Maddox had kept this secret from them? Or because he was trying to be a good scientist, skeptical to the end? He wasn't sure.

"We should be able to use ground launchers to send these bombs into the air as well," Maddox said.

Cross had a horrible image of apes hurling mudballs at tanks. He tried to shake it off.

"We have given this technology to all of the world governments," Maddox was saying, "and they are rapidly arming themselves. Between these bombs and Ms. Groopman's nanorescuers, we have a strong defense against the aliens."

Cross glanced at her. But that wasn't all. From what she had said before, they were making other plans as well. "Are we going to attack them before they get into orbit?"

"We haven't finalized any other plans, yet, Dr. Cross," Maddox said.

He bit his lower lip. He wanted to say to her that keeping secrets wasn't productive, that this time it was the humans against the aliens, not the U.S. against some other country. But he didn't. He'd had that fight with Maddox before—countless times—and it had done no good.

She looked at him for a long moment, as if expecting him to make the same old tired argument. When he didn't, she said, "Unless anyone has anything to add, I'd like to close this meeting. As I said before, we'll deal with details outside of this structure. Does anyone have anything major they'd like to say?"

There was a moment of silence. Maddox again looked at Cross. He would talk to her about the secrecy in private.

"Well, then," Maddox said. "There is only one more thing I need to discuss."

She paused, it seemed, for dramatic effect.

"This will be the last meeting of the Tenth Planet Project."

So that was why she had been looking at Cross. She had been preparing herself for his reaction. "This is the wrong time to break up the Project," he said. "We need the consortium of minds and information—"

"I know, Dr. Cross." Maddox smiled. "The problem is that we no longer have the luxury of time. These meetings take hours that I don't have and neither does anyone else on this extended team. Besides, with the unrest all over the world, getting together is taking longer and is less productive."

"But—"

"Let me finish," Maddox said.

He could have sworn her eyes twinkled. She had presented that news this way just to get him riled. He had been manipulated, and he was trying not to be angry about it.

"I agree that continuing to coordinate information from scientists and leaders from all over the world is important. I believe that it is crucial in these next twenty-nine days. But I think we must avail ourselves of technology and stop relying on face-to-face meetings. Instead, I think we need to work without such a rigorous meeting schedule."

Her words quieted Cross.

"What I would like to do is this." Again, she paused. She was tormenting him, and getting some enjoyment out of it. He hadn't realized that she actually liked sparring with him. "Dr. Cross, I want you to coordinate all of the information through this Tenth Planet Group, make sure each of us remains informed, and keep all of the channels open so that we are perhaps *more* informed than we've been."

Cross frowned. "I have good equipment, but it's not up to this many satellite links and—"

"I know," Maddox said. "That's why I've arranged for you to work out of the communications section of STScI's lab. Offices will be cleared for you by this afternoon, and additional equipment is already there. We have several assistants lined up to help you, although we know you'll want to bring in some of your own."

He was feeling railroaded and he wanted to protest, but he didn't. She was giving him what he had been asking for all along. Free-flowing information. Even more free-flowing than it had been. And he was going to coordinate it all.

"All right," Cross said. "How much setup will this take?"

"Most of it has already been done," Maddox said. "All of you should find e-mail in your links telling you how to stay in contact."

Britt squeezed Cross's hand. "At least we'll be in the same area now," she whispered.

He glanced at her. Had she known about these plans and not told him? He felt a flare of anger, then set it aside. He didn't like being out of the loop, and that was what he was reacting to. It wasn't Britt's fault. And Maddox was right. This was the best for all of them. Cross had taken a couple of much needed hours just to get to the meeting, and the meeting itself was taking a lot of time. He could speed up this process considerably.

"Now I am going to officially call an end to this last face-to-face meeting of the Tenth Planet Project." Maddox seemed to make eye contact with everyone on the screens as well as at the table. "Humankind has a great chance of surviving this war because of the work of everyone here. I, for one, am proud to be a part of this team."

She smiled at him, then went on. "I hope you will all avail yourselves of the new methods of communication. I expect to be hearing about all of your work regularly. And I hope that when we meet again, face to face, it will be for a worldwide victory celebration."

She slapped her hands on the table. "Meeting adjourned."

One by one the screens winked out.

Maddox stood. She started for the door, but Cross caught her arm.

"You blindsided me," he said.

"You're the one who wanted freer communication," she said.

"And I think it'll work," he said. "I think it's the right decision."

Her features softened just a bit. "Yet you're complaining."

He shook his head. "Not really."

He glanced at the others, making the look obvious, so that Maddox knew what he said was just for her. The remaining members of the Project were talking to Portia.

"There is one question that I have for you," Cross said. "You alluded to something twice in this meeting. First you said, 'Let me tell you what I can of our military plans.' This implies that there are plans you can't tell us about. And secondly, you dodged my question about other forms of attack. Why are you keeping secrets, General?"

Her smile faded. "Dr. Cross, it's always been military policy to keep things close to the chest."

"I know that," he said. "But this time things are different. We're not fighting other humans who are trying to discover our strategy and tactics. We're fighting creatures we've never seen before."

"I know," she said. "But the art of war is an ancient one. And it has always been contingent on secrets. We don't make decisions by committee in the military. All I can tell you is that we have other plans in the works. I am not at liberty to tell you—or anyone else here— what they are. Most of my direct subordinates don't know either."

"Wouldn't it be better to let us know?"

She shook her head. "We don't have systems in place for that sort of thing, and we don't have time to invent them. It's better to use tradition. The systems are in place and take no thought to implement. Right now, I'm staring down the barrel of a gun that will go off in exactly twenty-nine days. If I can carve out extra time in those twenty-nine days and not jeopardize our mission, I will. That includes using old methods because they already exist. It includes dissolving as many formal meetings as I can—not just with the Project, but with my own staff and others."

Her blue eyes were steely. Cross had never met anyone with such power in her gaze.

"I'll be honest with you, Dr. Cross. We have to cram months of work into the next few weeks. We can do it if we work at peak efficiency and on very little sleep. If we miss by so much as a hair, we lose. And I hate to lose."

"I don't think losing is an option, General."

"Neither do I, Dr. Cross," she said. "That's why I've gone to so much trouble to continue this group. You're going to run it now, Dr. Cross. No secrets, except the ones that someone chooses to withhold from you. Let the information flow."

He smiled.

"But don't waste my time having me read memos or getting redundant e-mail or watching dull vids. Boil it down, pass it on to the right parties, keep us all informed, but in a way that speeds things up rather than slows them down. Is that clear?"

"Yes, ma'am."

"Good." She nodded and started to walk away, then stopped as if she had another thought. "You do realize, Dr. Cross, why I put you in charge."

"To keep me out of trouble?" he joked.

She shook her head. "You're probably the only person in this entire project, perhaps the only person I've ever met, who can understand, coordinate, and communicate all of the various information that will flow from these people. I hope that you'll keep an open mind. I will. If one of your trademark hunches flows logically from this information, share it with me. I'll make sure you'll be heard."

Then she turned her back on him and left.

He watched the door close behind her. The shaded glass walls shimmered. He had been feeling the urgency of the aliens' arrival before, but now it seemed heightened.

And somehow, with Maddox's last minute charge, he felt as if the fate of the world rested on his shoulders.

October 12, 2018
9:22 A.M. Central Daylight Time

29 Days Until Second Harvest

Kara's feet hurt. At dawn, she had walked to the Loop, hoping to find a train that would take her somewhere close to home. All she had wanted to do was get on the Red Line, or even the Purple Line. The Red had an extension all the way to Lake Forest. It was the line she had taken the night before, before everything got crazy.

But it hadn't happened.

She had arrived to find the entire downtown section,

from the Daley Center to the Sears Tower, filled with broken glass, destroyed cars, and small fires. Not many rioters were still active, although there was a lot of looting going on.

She had walked the filthy concrete stairs up to the El at the first station she saw. It was on the corner of Washington and Dearborn. But as she peeked over the top, she realized she didn't want to go any farther.

A train was askew on the tracks, doors open, the interior destroyed. No one was on the platform, and the eerie emptiness terrified her. She couldn't even hear the rumble of a far-off train.

The booth had been knocked over, the electronic turnstiles destroyed.

At that moment, she had realized she wasn't taking an El home, and she'd started to shake.

She wasn't going to cry. She had survived so far. She wasn't going to let this get to her.

And she hadn't.

She was walking through the mess down Randolph to Lake Michigan. Lake Forest was on the lake—more than forty miles away, but on the lake—and she would walk it if she had to.

She was tired and cold and hungry. She had never spent a night outdoors before—not without a tent or family or friends. Sometime around midnight, she had crawled down some steps that led to a boarded-up door and wedged herself as far against the stone wall as possible. The sidewalk was above her, and from it she could hear the screams and shouts of people as they ran by.

The sounds of breaking glass faded, though, as the night went on—probably because there were few windows left. And the voices died down as the looting ceased. Once, she thought she caught the acrid scent of smoke, and she peeked out of her hiding place, afraid that the fire was nearby.

A car, upside down, its wheels moving like the feet of an upended turtle, had a fire on its undercarriage. But the flames hadn't looked like they'd spread, and she had eased back into her hiding place.

She knew she had slept, but that was only because she had bounced awake as her head slipped against the stone. Her dreams had been as bad as the night around her.

She had tried everything. She had searched for a cab, waited for the bus, and tried to get into some of the nearby hotels. The hotels had locked their doors. No people could get in and no guests could get out. She had pounded and screamed, and once, a security guard had come to the door. All he had done was tell her to go away.

Finally, when she'd found her safe place at the bottom of the stairs, she had used her wrist'puter to call her father. He had answered on the first ring, relief so deep in his voice when he realized it was her that it took her a moment to tell him what was happening.

She hadn't realized how worried he would be. She had thought he wouldn't even know she was gone. Her mother's voice had echoed in the background, also worried.

Kara had told her father where she was, what had

happened, and had urged him to get her. He had promised he would be there within the hour. But a half an hour later her 'puter vibrated against her wrist. She answered.

Her father was on the line. The roads were closed into the city. The police had formed barricades. He had been told he could go around them if he dared, but most people who did had their cars hijacked or worse.

He asked if she was all right and if she was in a safe place. She didn't know how to answer him. Finally she told him she was as safe as she could be.

He wasn't satisfied. He offered to have her go to one of his colleagues' condos on Lake Shore Drive, but she told him she was afraid to walk there. She was also afraid that the building would be closed, just like the hotels were. Still, he made her take his friend's name and address in case she had to leave her spot.

Her father offered to stay on the link all night, to keep her company, but his voice made her weepy and fearful. She was better off on her own, or so she had told him. When he finally hung up, she almost dialed him back, but didn't let herself. She had to get through the night on her own.

And now she had.

When she had walked to the Loop at dawn it was with the hope that the trains were repaired. All night she had heard gunshots, but the worst of the rioting had eased. As she walked, she still saw looters, but they didn't care about her.

No one seemed to care about her, now that she was grubby and filthy. She kept her sleeve buttoned over her wrist'puter, her only link to the real world, and she had stuffed her earrings and necklace in her pockets. She looked like any other street kid out to get into trouble, or so she hoped.

Now she was walking north on Lake Shore Drive. From Randolph to the Chicago River, the streets were deserted. There was no sign of anyone or anything, and no sign of trouble. Somehow that made her even more nervous than movement had.

But once she crossed the river into Streeterville, she heard screams and shouts again. There was smoke coming from her left—the entire Magnificent Mile seemed to be aflame. Apparently things had gotten worse since she had walked to the Loop.

She had been walking for hours and she hadn't even gotten as far north as she had been the night before. She was tired and hungry and her shoes pinched. She was tempted to go inside one of the destroyed businesses and grab a bottle of water. Who would know?

Who would care? In a month none of this would matter. Nothing would matter.

But that still didn't stop her from wanting to go home.

She had to find some shelter so she could call her dad again and tell him she was walking. Maybe when she got farther away from downtown, he would be able to pick her up.

It had been so dumb for her to leave home. She hadn't realized until she had done it that home was where she wanted to be. If she only had twenty-nine days left to live, she wanted to be with her family, not running in the street breaking things and stealing.

Maybe for the next twenty-nine days, she and her parents could pretend like nothing was happening. Maybe they could barricade themselves into their house, eat good meals and listen to music or watch vids. Maybe, if they worked at it hard enough, the end would come and they wouldn't even know.

It was better than going like this.

It was better than destroying everything around.

Everything was going to be gone soon enough. She didn't want to be one of the people who helped speed up the end.

3

October 12, 2018
4:56 P.M. Eastern Daylight Time

29 Days Until Second Harvest

The Roosevelt Room was crowded and hot. The autumnal centerpiece in the middle of the long conference table gave off the scent of decaying leaves. It made Secretary of State Doug Mickelson want to sneeze. He'd been fighting allergies all day. The weather was surprisingly warm for October, and his hay fever, which was usually the worst in September, had lingered into this month. It made his head feel full, and despite the allergy medication he was on, he didn't feel quite himself.

He needed to be doing the best job of his life right now, and when he had gone to his allergist the day before, he had asked that the allergist make all the symptoms go away.

I'm not God, Doug, the allergist had said. *If I were,*

I wouldn't be messing with your sinus cavities. I'd make those alien ships disappear.

Everyone on the planet would make those ships disappear if they could. Mickelson tried not to concentrate on them, but he was constantly aware of them—as if they were a storm bearing down on a particularly beautiful day.

Right now, he had most of his attention focused on the final draft of the president's speech. He was supposed to vet it to get rid of "potential international problems." The problems he was searching for were not with content—the world leaders had already spoken to Franklin and knew what the speech was about. They had, in fact, chosen him to give it.

What Mickelson was looking for was offensive language. He and a battery of international experts from the various foreign desks throughout the White House were going over the speech line by line. The press secretary and a battalion of the president's speech writers were in the room as well, all making notes.

President Franklin himself was sitting at the head of the conference table, a red pen in hand, marking on a hard copy before him. He was the only person not working off a palm-sized screen, and Mickelson actually envied him for it.

The door to the room opened, and Grace Lopez, the president's chief of staff, looked in. She was a short round woman with curly gray hair and a manner that made Mickelson want to snap to attention.

"Everyone's here," she said. "All the networks are

set up. They've blocked time. You promised a speech at five sharp."

"Nearly there, Grace," Franklin said.

She sighed loudly and closed the door.

Franklin raised his head only after she left. The worry lines around his dark eyes seemed even deeper than usual. "I want this speech to be perfect and it's not going to be, is it?"

Mickelson opened his mouth to say that perfection no longer mattered, that the longer the president waited the more torn up the world would become, but at that moment, Franklin said, "Screw it."

Everyone in the room froze.

Franklin looked at them. "We're going to offend someone. That can't be my concern right now. If a nation doesn't like the way I say something, screw them. Their own leaders can try to clean up the mess."

He stood. Mickelson held out a hand to stop him. "Mr. President," Mickelson said, "just let us finish going through this—"

"Nice try, Doug," Franklin said. "But it's time we stop going through the political motions. If we dither too much, we won't make our deadline. And this is one deadline that is aptly named, don't you think?"

Dead . . . line. The pun made Mickelson shudder almost as much as the thought of dealing with any diplomatic crisis that came from the speech.

"Right now I'm expected to speak for the world. Well, they're going to have to like the sound of my voice. I'm tired of altering it for anyone." And with that, Franklin grabbed the papers off the table and left the room.

"Shit," Patrick Aldrich, the press secretary, said. "Someone stop him."

"How can we stop him?" one of the speechwriters asked. "He's the leader of the free world."

"It's not done," Aldrich said.

"I think the president thinks it is," Mickelson said. "And if you don't want this to become even more of a disaster, you might want to load the speech as is onto the TelePrompTer and make sure that everything's ready across the hall."

"Shit," Aldrich said again, and ran outside.

One of the speechwriters looked at Mickelson. "That's diplomacy?"

Mickelson grinned. "Hell, no. That's passing the buck."

He left the Roosevelt Room with its heat and smelly floral arrangement and crossed the wide hallway into the Oval Office. He had only seen the office like this once before, on June 15, the night that President Franklin made his famous "We Have Risen Up in Self-Defense" speech.

That speech, Franklin had believed, would be the defining moment of his career. At the time, Mickelson had agreed. Now, he thought that tonight's speech was more important.

No one had expected the world to erupt into so much chaos. Well, he hadn't. Tavi Bernstein, the director of the FBI had warned that this would happen on an internal level. She had predicted the bombing of the Capitol Building, too.

He slipped into the far side of the Oval Office, near the white couches where he had been during so many meetings. The other advisers stood near the walls, as they had during the Rise Up speech. Vid reporters from dozens of networks had set up on the space between the partners desk and the couches. The eagle emblem of the United States, with the words *E Pluribus Unum*, was completely hidden beneath expensive shoes.

Someone had placed lights around the front of the partners desk, and Grace had closed the drapes. Next to the American flag were flags of the European Union, the African Nations, Russia, and several other countries. That had been Mickelson's idea. He wanted a visual symbol that Franklin was speaking for all of them.

The vid reporters with their tiny handhelds and their chip-sized mikes, tried to be inconspicuous while they waited. The only person who was missing was Franklin. How could he have disappeared so quickly?

Mickelson scanned the room. Aldrich entered through one of the side doors. Lopez was missing, too. Maybe Franklin had pulled that little stunt in the Roosevelt Room just so that he could get this started on time.

Either that or he was in his study, rewriting the speech himself.

Mickelson cringed inwardly. He was as worried

about this speech as Franklin was, maybe more so. Mickelson had been all over the world in the last few weeks, and he knew that everything was close to boiling over. And now the riots and the unrest that had started since the announcement that there were alien ships returning was like the steam that appeared before a volcano erupted.

Franklin's speech would either contain the eruption or force it to happen tonight. Mickelson hoped that Franklin could channel all that pent-up energy and direct it where it needed to be—against the aliens.

Perhaps that was why they were all tinkering with the speech, because they all knew how important it was, and how hard it would be to get it right. Perhaps that was what had irritated Franklin the most. Ultimately, this moment was his.

The door from the president's study opened and Grace Lopez entered. She was a small dynamo making her way into the fray. She beckoned Aldrich, who joined her. As they walked, she whispered something to him. He nodded. They stopped in front of the partners desk and she held up her hands, the sign for silence.

Mickelson smiled. Except for whispered conversation, the room had been silent. No one had dared talk—it was as if the night were too solemn for even casual conversation.

Surprisingly, it was Aldrich who spoke. "The president will be here in a matter of moments. He will make his speech and then leave. There will be no time for questions. This is not the place for them."

Mickelson heard some groaning from the press, but no one raised a hand and asked for the policy to be changed even though Aldrich seemed braced for that. Lopez was watching the door to the president's study. After a moment, she elbowed Aldrich and got out of the way.

"Ladies and gentlemen," he said as if they were in the larger, better equipped press conference room, "the president of the United States."

Mickelson noted that the final stage of lighting did not go on until Aldrich moved out of the way. The international press did not broadcast the introduction— which was probably the right move.

Franklin walked across the room with a dignity that Mickelson had only seen in the man once before—on inauguration day. On that day, Franklin had later said, he felt the history and weight of the office for the first time.

He clearly felt it now.

Franklin sat at the partners desk, placed some papers on the top, then pressed a button on the side. A small clear screen rose from the modern protector that had been placed over the desk by the previous administration.

Mickelson winced. Franklin was using his own TelePrompTer. He had revised the speech. Mickelson hoped he didn't lose any of the content in the translation. That would definitely cause an international incident.

"Citizens of Earth," Franklin said, holding up the hard copy, an old-fashioned habit that he still favored.

"I come to you tonight not as the president of the United States, but as a spokesman for all the world's leaders. We have a plan that will allow us to defend ourselves against the threat posed by the tenth planet, a plan that we are going to share with you tonight."

So far so good, Mickelson thought. The opening was slightly different than originally written, but it sounded warm and personal.

"I am speaking to you right now as a representative because we, the world leaders, believed that you should hear about what we are going to do from one voice. After my speech, your own country's leader will speak, explaining how the plan will affect your individual country. But for this moment, we are one world. We are united in our opposition to the threat posed by the tenth planet. We speak with one voice—a human voice. A voice that the tenth planet will learn to respect."

Mickelson felt a shiver run down his back. Here was where Franklin deviated from the plan. He was going to sound tougher than the speechwriters had thought he should. The international experts and the speechwriters were afraid that a tough U.S. president would alienate the other countries.

Mickelson hadn't agreed, but hadn't really argued his point either. He didn't know the fine art of speechmaking. He did most of his diplomatic work on the fly.

"I know that all of you are frightened and panicked. You have all seen the images of last April's destruction over and over again. But let me tell you about what we have done to the tenth planet." Franklin's dark eyes shone in the bright light. "We have hit them with nuclear weapons, destroying some of their shielding around their planet. The destruction we have caused to their surface would be the same as if someone had destroyed over half of the United States. In other words, we have hurt them worse than they have hurt us.

"Why are they returning? Because they have no choice."

Franklin went on to outline why the scientists believed the tenth planet harvested Earth. As he did that, and as he told the citizens of the world why this was an important detail, Mickelson examined the faces. So far everyone in the room seemed rapt, even the reporters. It seemed as if information was what they had lacked, and getting it satisfied something, something they hadn't even known they needed.

"We have no choice," Franklin said. "We are *not* some other planet's food source. We will defend ourselves. And we will win."

Mickelson felt his heart leap with the words. They were Franklin's words and they were the right ones. Mickelson no longer worried about the changes that Franklin had made in the speech.

"We need the cooperation of every person in the world for this plan to succeed. We must stop fighting each other and look toward the heavens. That's where the threat is coming from. And if we stand united, we can defeat that threat."

Every time he repeated that, Mickelson noted, people in the Oval Office stood taller.

"Now to the plan," Franklin said. "We have established safe zones so that no one need die in the horrible manner that we saw last April. Because the aliens are coming here for food and supplies, we are certain they will not attack the deserts. Nor will they send spacecraft over the ocean. We have established places in the deserts where people may stay. We will also launch every available oceangoing ship, and there will be room on all of them for passengers.

"The most important safe zones, though, will be our cities. Every major city on Earth will be safe from alien attack."

Mickelson saw some of the reporters frown. They hadn't expected this.

"We have developed a technology that will destroy the alien harvesters. Because we are on a tight deadline, and we only recently discovered this solution, we have limited amounts of it. We had to choose how best to allocate it. We decided to deploy it in the major cities and the surrounding areas within a twenty-mile radius."

Mickelson sighed with relief. Franklin had not mentioned exactly what the defense was, nor had he said that it would be dusted over the cities. The advisers had disagreed about that, but most of the world leaders were afraid that average citizens, hearing about more tiny machines from the skies, would be afraid to come into the cities.

The leaders had decided that it was better to be vague. Franklin hadn't agreed with that at first, when Mickelson had presented it to him. But at least he had listened.

Franklin was saying, "Anyone living outside this defense area must move to shelters inside the protected areas. Reporters are being given lists of protected cities and maps of each protected area. These maps will also air after this speech and can be downloaded on any link."

The Web sites were being activated as Franklin spoke. None of the sites had been online until that moment.

Mickelson leaned against the cool wall. So many precautions to prevent an even worse panic than the one that was happening right now.

"Individually, you can do a thousand things to help us prepare for this mass influx into the cities. We will need help setting up shelters, preparing food, coordinating things. The details on how you may join this effort will follow this speech and may also be downloaded. The information is located by city."

Aldrich hovered near the door to the study. He was holding packets, with all the important information. Mickelson hadn't even seen him get it.

"If you live in the desert or are within a twenty-mile radius of any major city, you will be safe from alien attack," Franklin was saying. "If you are not, make plans to get to one of those locations in the next twenty-nine days."

Franklin leaned forward. "I have promised you that we will fight back. Indeed, we already have. The attack we made on the tenth planet was only the first step in a coordinated effort that began as soon as we realized that the tenth planet existed."

Mickelson felt his shoulders stiffen. Again, Franklin was off the script. He wasn't going to mention the Tenth Planet Project, was he? Conspiracy nuts would hate to know just how many people were involved and how coordinated the effort was.

"Because of our planning," Franklin said, "we have found ways to attack the alien ships. We have conducted tests on the downed alien crafts and know that our plans will work. Every plane that can be equipped to fight will be in the air in the coming battle with the new technology and weapons. The aliens will not know what hit them."

"Good," one of the reporters near Mickelson whispered.

Mickelson suppressed a grin. He hoped other people were having the same reaction. Across the room, he saw Tavi Bernstein glance at him. Apparently, she, too, had been worried that Franklin was going to mention the Project and was relieved that he hadn't.

Franklin's intensity seemed to have grown. "Our plan is defensive—we will protect our people and we will attack any ship that comes into our atmosphere— and offensive. We will fight the aliens from space.

"Let me say this again: *we will win this fight.*"

Mickelson actually found himself nodding. He felt like he was in a high school pep rally and he felt the president's magic working on him.

Franklin paused for a moment as if he were going to say something grave. Mickelson's heart pounded. He hoped that Franklin wasn't going to ruin the mood he had just created.

"The only way for us to succeed in our plan is to work together," Franklin said. His tone was both gentle and chastising. "All rioting must stop immediately. We need cities to house all of our people. Our enemy is coming from space. We must work together, as one race, the human race, to fight back. We do not have the time or the resources to fight among ourselves."

Mickelson nodded. That was well done. It wasn't too harsh and it wasn't too specific.

Franklin had already declared martial law when the rioting started, but now he was going to enforce it to the fullest of his powers. He was going to use the armed forces to keep the peace and set up shelters. Anyone caught looting or rioting would probably be shot.

The argument was that people needed to know this in order to stop. But Mickelson had said that U.S. policies would distract from the international nature of the speech. Mickelson knew full well that some countries would think the U.S. response too harsh, while others would think it too soft.

This issue had been settled before Franklin got frustrated. The U.S. policies would be announced after the speech, not by Franklin—who didn't want to dilute his message—but by the vice president. The vice president's presence would send a subtle message to Americans that while the president was tending to world business, the vice president would watch over the home front.

It was supposed to be reassuring. Mickelson hoped

that the people of the U.S. trusted the vice president more than he did.

"Until now," Franklin was saying, "you had only vague promises that we were working on solutions. Tonight, I have shared our plans with you. Our goals— the goals of every citizen on Earth—are exactly the same.

"Whenever you find something difficult—and the next few weeks will be difficult—look at the sky. Remember what you saw last April. And do your part to defeat our joint enemy.

"For the next twenty-nine days, we are not individuals. We are a race, united against a common enemy. We must do everything we can to save our planet—our home. We have the plans in place. Let's work together to achieve them."

With his left hand, Franklin turned over the hard copy he had been holding.

"We will win this battle. We will preserve the Earth for our children and our children's children. Our planet will be ours once again."

Franklin stared into the cameras, and after a moment, the lights shut off.

The silence echoed for the longest time and then someone in the press corps started to clap.

The clapping continued and grew throughout the room. No one was getting this on tape. This was a spontaneous outgrowth of the speech.

Mickelson found himself clapping, too.

In this room, filled with the ghosts of ex-presidents

and a history so deep that he didn't like to contemplate it, Mickelson had just experienced something he had never thought he would feel again.

He had felt hope.

October 12, 2018
5:28 P.M. Eastern Daylight Time

29 Days Until Second Harvest

Leo Cross had two reactions to the president's speech: one was an overwhelmingly positive emotional reaction—he wanted to get up and cheer at several points in the speech—and the other was a cool intellectual reaction, filled with skepticism and doubt. He didn't say anything, though, as President Franklin spoke. Instead he watched Britt, who stared at the screens intently.

They were in his new office on the second floor of Britt's lab. The office was small and had clearly been cleaned out just for him. Dozens of screens covered the small walls, and he had access to even more screens through his desk. He had never been in a place so wired in his life. There were several systems here, each with a different level of security hardwired in. He could have several different conversations, at several different security clearances, all at the same time.

Britt had assured him that the systems were easy to

use. He hoped so. He didn't have the time to catch himself up on the newest technologies. If it got too complicated, he'd go to his own media room at home.

The room smelled faintly of dust and fresh plastic. There were boxes outside the door—apparently from the room's previous occupant—and some of the details hadn't been finished before Cross arrived. His lamps hadn't been plugged in. Someone had not finished assembling his chair and he had nearly fallen off the loose seat onto the floor. But those were minor irritations.

He had spent the afternoon getting ready to coordinate the largest information feed in the history of the project.

And then he had tuned all of his screens to Franklin's speech. After a few moments of that, though, he had shut off most of them. He liked Franklin; the man was a bit too charming and too political, but he was a good president. But more than one of him repeated on various screens was completely overwhelming.

As the speech started, Britt had joined Cross. He liked being this close to her. If he hadn't gotten this assignment, they would have been watching the speech in separate parts of the city.

When the speech ended and the maps appeared on the screens, she touched his desktop and muted the sound. She knew the systems here better than Cross did.

"What'd you think?" Her reaction was obvious. Her

cheeks were flushed and her eyes were bright. She had been inspired.

Cross wasn't sure he wanted to ruin that reaction. Britt had been getting increasingly morose the longer this had gone on.

"I thought it was an effective speech," Cross said. "I think it'll accomplish most of Franklin's goals."

Britt must have caught the skepticism in his tone. "Are they different from ours?"

Cross let out a small sigh. They had had these kinds of conversations before. A large part of his archaeology training had included a study of history, and a large part of the study of history had included analysis of political systems.

Politicians in times of crisis had several jobs, but their main job was to rally the civilians behind the cause, to make certain the troops remained loyal, and to stem unrest at home. Franklin's speech did all three of those things.

"Leo?" Britt put her fingers on his arm. They were warm and dry, and felt good against his skin. "What's bothering you?"

"Some things he said."

The brightness in her eyes dimmed slightly, just as he was afraid it would.

"Not," he said quickly, "because he's wrong or anything. I think we have a good shot at fighting back. I think this speech will go a long way toward settling the unrest and I think we'll be able to keep people looking toward the skies. I think all of that's good."

"Me, too," Britt said. "So what else is going on?"

Cross put his hand over her fingers. "When a politician gives a speech you have to listen to the words he chooses and the details he leaves out. He's going to try to grab your emotions—"

"Franklin did that."

"Yes, and he needed to," Cross said. "This was probably the best speech of his career. But he also gave out what seemed to be a large amount of information."

"You mean it wasn't?"

He wasn't going to be able to get out of this conversation. Cross sighed. "Well, I got a piece of information out of Franklin that I couldn't get out of Maddox."

"What was that?"

"That we are going to fight in space. That the fight will be an offensive one. But he hasn't told us the plan."

"Why should he? This was a speech to the general public."

Cross nodded. "My point exactly. You and I feel like we got a lot of information out of the speech because we already know a lot of this information. I'd love to know how other people reacted to it."

"I'll poll the lab," Britt said, standing. Apparently she didn't want him to spoil her reaction to the speech either.

"You don't have to. We'll find out public reaction soon enough." Cross stood, too, and kissed her gently. "I've got a lot of setting up to do. I want to be able to contact most of the group later tonight. Maybe you and

86

I can catch a bite of pizza together when the lab does its nightly order?"

"We haven't been able to do that since the rioting started. We're stuck with canned cafeteria food."

"Uck," Cross said. "All right. How about a date over Spam?"

She grinned. "You're on. Maybe I'll make you my special Spam and tuna surprise."

He grimaced and ushered her out. Then he leaned against the door, letting the disquiet that had begun during the speech settle in.

Franklin had sworn that people would be safe in the cities. But Cross had done some checking after Portia's plea to the Project that morning. Even her best-case scenario wasn't quite accurate.

The factories making the nanorescuers were working at full capacity, but they weren't producing the numbers needed. The other factories that were coming on-line in the next few days would help, but they wouldn't get up to full speed right away. It was going to take luck to provide enough nanorescuers to cover every major city, its suburbs, and the twenty-mile radius around that.

He ran a hand through his hair and looked at his new, sterile office. He longed to go outside and listen to the people on the street. He wanted to know if anyone else had figured out what Portia caught so quickly in the meeting that morning: that the president was saying that most of the planet would be undefended.

The cities combined were only a small area. The rest

of the planet, from the rain forests to the veldts, would be unprotected.

And then there was the issue of the current unrest. Franklin purposely hadn't touched on the U.S. response, but Cross had been hearing the announcements all afternoon. The president had declared martial law and he hadn't been the only leader to do so. For the first time in Cross's lifetime, most of the governments around the world had declared martial law. Freedoms that most Americans—most of the civilized world—took for granted had suddenly disappeared.

If the world survived—and Cross had to believe it would—it would come out of this battle a place he no longer recognized.

He pushed away from the door and walked to his desk. So much work and so many decisions. He was still in the center of it all. In fact, he was probably more in the center than he had been since the first attack.

Maddox had done him a favor. She had given him control again. She had trusted him more than she had let on.

He hoped he was worthy of the trust. He was going into this tired and stressed, and worried that no matter what they all did, the aliens would have some surprises that they couldn't plan for.

It was his job to make sure there were no surprises.

He would do all he could.

At least Britt was nearby.

A dinner of Spam and canned tuna was worth suffering through if he had Britt across from him. He smiled. In fact, all of this was worthwhile as long as Britt was at his side.

October 12, 2018
5:18 P.M. Central Daylight Time

29 Days Until Second Harvest

Kara Willis hung up and put her hand over her wrist'puter. She wanted to keep talking to her father, but knew that it would be better to wait in silence. Let him drive. Let him get here.

She sat on a rusted swing in Rogers School Park. A breeze from nearby Lake Michigan caught her, bringing the scents of fish and brine. Still, that was better than the smoke she'd been smelling all day.

The park was mostly empty, although the bundles of garbage and the remains of campfires showed her that a lot of people had slept here the night before. She suspected they would do the same thing tonight.

She didn't want to be here when they did.

Kara had managed to walk here, nearly to Evanston, dodging looters and rioters along the way. The day had been difficult. She was tired and sore from sleeping on the ground; her feet hurt because she was wearing the wrong shoes; and she was incredibly hungry.

She had found water fountains along the way, especially in the parks near the lake. Fortunately the fountains hadn't been turned off for the winter yet. At the first one, she drank and drank and drank, thinking she would never get her fill.

But water wasn't a great substitute for food, and her stomach ached. She had never gone without eating this long before—and she had certainly never walked this much before.

She had made it to Rogers Park just south of Evanston before she decided to call her father again. He said that he probably could get that close to the city and that she should stay put and wait for him. Watch the president's speech, he said.

Kara hadn't known the president was going to make a speech. She didn't know if she cared about it either. But she had a choice between watching the speech and counting the seconds until her father arrived, so she turned on the video/audio on her wrist'puter and watched as best she could.

A few blocks away where Rogers met Ridge, she could hear screaming and more breaking glass. She had thought all the glass in the city had been destroyed by now, but she had been wrong. Gunshots echoed and she noticed that she had stopped cringing. She was actually getting used to them.

She noted all of that during the speech, and yet she found herself involved in the president's words. Not enough to get up and tell those crazy people a few blocks away to settle down. But enough to hope that they would listen and look toward the skies.

The president believed they could win. He knew more than she did. She hoped he was right.

When her father picked her up, she really didn't

want to look in his eyes and see that hopelessness, that sorrow that he had even brought her into the world. She couldn't face any more despair.

When the president finished, she realized that the entire neighborhood was silent. Did everyone else hear him? Or were other people coming out now, telling the rioters that it was over, that they had a job to do?

She didn't know.

But things were slowing down around her.

Then she heard some more breaking glass, and a loud male laugh that sounded out of control or drunk and she realized that the people on the street hadn't all gotten the word.

With shaking fingers, she had dialed her father again. And this time, she caught him on the road. He was taking back streets, he told her, and it would take longer than usual, but he would be able to pick her up. She warned him about the noises at Rogers and Ridge, assured him that she was safe, and hung up.

And ever since, she had been rocking back and forth on the swing. She would look at the sky—deceptively blue and pretty above her—and the lake, also blue and pretty on this sunny October evening.

When she was little, her parents had taken her on a Great Lakes cruise, and they had stayed at a hotel on Mackinac Island. She had taken a bike ride around the island, fascinated that people lived there, stunned that the only way off was by boat or small plane. She had wondered how people had allowed themselves to be trapped like that.

She hadn't realized, until yesterday, that Earth was

an island, too. If someone wanted to hurt the Earth, she couldn't leave it. She didn't have the power.

She was trapped here.

She sighed and clutched the rusted chain of the swing. The president said that they would survive. They were in a city; they would be safe. He had promised.

But, a few months ago, he had said that the attack on the tenth planet was a victory. That had felt like a promise, too. One he had failed to keep.

She wrapped her hands around the chain, feeling the cold metal dig into her skin. The breeze off the lake felt good. It tickled her face and caressed her skin.

A gunshot echoed off a nearby building. The sound was close, but not that close.

Yet.

Her father would be here soon. She could hang on until he arrived.

She glanced at the lake again, and then at the sky. She believed her father would come, no matter what the odds. She believed he had the power to save her.

She had to have that same kind of belief about the president. He knew more about what was happening than she did. He said he had hope.

She had to believe him.

FIRST BATTLE

4

November 9, 2018
4:23 Universal Time

1 Day Until Second Harvest

Commander Cicoi clung to his command post, his upper tentacles flat on the controls. He had changed the view shown through the walls of the warship. Instead of magnifying the target, it showed the actual space around them.

The third planet was a small bright ball in space. They were headed directly toward it. The blue-and-white planet seemed so harmless from this distance, yet thinking of it made Cicoi's eyestalks quiver.

He had no idea what the creatures of the third planet planned this time. As the ships traveled, he had asked his command staff to come up with suggestions. They had used information gathered from past harvest Passes about the nature of the creatures.

As primitives, the creatures had been aggressive and inventive, once burning an entire small section of their own planet instead of allowing the Malmurian harvest on its Second Pass. In those days, long ago, the creatures had been willing to destroy their own home rather than let anyone else do so.

Cicoi wondered if they would do that again. Only this time the creatures had developed into a spacefaring society. Would they think to destroy the entire planet so that the Malmuria would not get food?

The attack on Malmur suggested that the creatures were still aggressive. And not willing to give up easily. Cicoi wished he had the luxury of unlimited energy. If he did, he would bring the creatures to submission first and then harvest the planet.

But he did not have that luxury, and so he had to follow a carefully ordered plan.

The Commanders of the North and Center would move their ships to their assigned positions. Center would harvest one location in the third planet's northern hemisphere, while North and Cicoi would harvest two different locations in the southern hemisphere.

These locations had no creature population centers. Cicoi believed that to be a mistake.

Still reviewing decisions already made?

The whisper inside Cicoi's mind belonged to the Elder. Cicoi hated the way the Elder slipped inside him and heard his innermost thoughts. Cicoi had learned, on this trip, to answer the Elder silently. The first few times he had spoken aloud and startled his own staff.

I believe we must attack the creatures first, Cicoi

thought. His upper tentacles floated slightly in his distress. He had to work to bring them down.

He did not see the Elder, but that meant nothing. The Elder often camouflaged his dark ghostly shape against the blackness of space.

They will expect that. We must take food first.

We have two other harvests on this Pass. We can take food after we subdue them.

You have never fought a war, the Elder said. *The greatest weapon is surprise.*

How can we surprise creatures we do not understand?

Cicoi felt an amusement not his own touch him. *We understand them. You have been analyzing them. We have observed them for many Passes now. We know what they are.*

Yet they managed to surprise us, Cicoi thought.

Because they developed rapidly during your last sleep. We had not expected that. But they are still the same creatures. Only their technology differs.

I hope you're right, Cicoi thought.

But you do not believe that I am. The Elder floated in front of him, a darkness blotting the small blue-and-white planet at the cone of the ship.

What I believe does not matter, Cicoi thought, pocketing all but two of his eyestalks in respect. *I will follow orders. I will complete our mission.*

Food first. The Elder moved closer to him. *Survival before all else. That is your strategy. Survival first. Revenge second.*

You think I want revenge?

Don't you? The Elder's thought was a cold one. *It is only natural.*

And then he floated away.

Cicoi removed the eight eyestalks from their pockets and sent them in different positions so that he could monitor his staff. The Elder always unsettled him. He hated it. He wanted to feel in command of himself as well as the mission. He needed certainty now, not doubt.

Revenge. Cicoi turned his front four eyestalks toward the blue-and-white planet. The creatures—primitives not one sleep ago—had destroyed pods, ruined nestlings, hurt brood females. They had caused severe damage to Malmur, something he thought could never happen.

And they had prevented him from carrying out his duty as a Malmuria. They had destroyed so many of his people that he had to live with his failure instead of recycling his energy as he should do.

Perhaps he wanted revenge. But even more, he worried about another failure. His first had cost Malmur so much.

Maybe that was why the Elder was unsettling him, so that Cicoi would think along the correct track when he began the attack.

It would happen soon. The trip was almost over. And he had to make the right choices.

Survival first.

Revenge second.

But there would be revenge. Even the Elder had promised that.

November 9, 2018
10:23 A.M. Eastern Standard Time

1 Day Until Second Harvest

Leo Cross had a headache. And his stomach, filled with caffeine and the remains of the world's greasiest burger, was making sounds of distress. He had a report on the aliens to finish and send to General Maddox, and he had a lot more information to collate. Then he had to oversee the last few hours of work in the Tenth Planet Project.

All of the research was coming in now, of course. He had asked the Project members to report as they worked—and many of them had—but most of them kept working right to the deadline and beyond. The deadline was yesterday, but Cross's links had been beeping all day with updates and changes and revised reports.

He had five assistants who were coordinating the process with him, but he was determined to do everything himself. He hadn't forgotten what Maddox had said to him less than a month before.

She wanted him to see all the information so that he would have one of his famous hunches. She had actually given him a direct link to her office in case he got one during the battle.

He hadn't had a hunch yet, only a bad case of eye-strain and a growing wish for a long night's sleep. But he knew he wouldn't sleep, probably not more than a few snatched hours here and there over the next week.

If the world made it through the next week.

But the world had survived so far, and sometimes he thought that was a small miracle. The president's speech had been a major turning point. It had only occurred twenty-eight days ago, but it seemed as if that was years ago. Time stretched when a person was as busy as Cross had been.

The speech had accomplished a lot of things. It had stopped the worst of the rioting. In fact, in the U.S., all of the rioting had ended. Some countries hadn't been able to contain theirs, though, and thousands of deaths had resulted worldwide. In several Third World nations, governments had toppled. Unlike times past, that had barely caused a ripple on the worldwide stage.

As Franklin had commanded, everyone was looking skyward. They weren't going to worry about internal matters if they could avoid it.

Here in the States, people were following the rules, for the most part, honoring curfews and moving to safe zones. There were scuffles as more and more people crowded the major cities. But those who couldn't abide crowded conditions had gone to the deserts.

Cross knew there were millions of people world-wide, maybe hundreds of millions, who were gambling that the aliens wouldn't attack their little bit of unprotected land, but no one was paying much attention to them either. The attitude across the world seemed to be one that was expressed by a little British boy in a vid clip that had aired repeatedly in the last week:

Either come join the party or fend for yourself.

Not that living in the cities was a party right now. The overcrowding was phenomenal. Every city had different rules for dealing with it.

Washington's were strict: a person with any unused bedrooms had to open his house to strangers; homeowners on an acre or more of land had to permit tents and temporary shelters on the lawn.

Cross's home was overrun with people he barely knew—former students of Bradshaw's, friends of Portia's, and shirttail relatives he hadn't seen for years. He'd locked off the basement and his bedroom where he had most of his personal papers, and spent most of his time here at the office, away from the hubbub in his old sanctuary.

When he needed a bed, he usually went to Britt's. She had a one-bedroom apartment, and wasn't under orders to share.

He usually didn't see her at the apartment, though. She was spending as much time here at the lab as he was. Her lab had become the clearinghouse for all the telemetry coming in from the probes and telescopes as they tracked the alien fleet coming toward Earth. He went to her section of the building every day, secretly hoping to find out the aliens had turned back.

Of course, they hadn't.

He leaned back in his chair and rubbed his eyes. He needed more caffeine. He wondered if it would help calm his troubled stomach or if it would make things worse. If he had been keeping track of what he had been eating, he would have been fine, but he had been living Britt's lifestyle lately—eat what you found; sleep when you could; survive on coffee if possible. He hadn't even done that in college. It felt almost indecent now.

He stood and stretched, hearing bones in his spine crack. He had no idea how long he had been sitting. The last time he remembered going to a window had been yesterday. He had watched as the first dusting planes had flown over this section of D.C., raining Portia's nanorescuers onto the city.

The dusting process had caused minor panics worldwide. Even though people had been warned, the dark nanorescuers falling from the sky looked so much like the dark cloud of alien nanoharvesters that many people fled in hysteria. When the little rescuers didn't hurt anyone, people calmed down. But it showed Cross at least how volatile the world still was.

He had to admit he'd felt a bit of déjà vu himself as he watched the tiny particles stream from the belly of the planes. He had watched the footage of the nanoharvesters just like everyone else, and the images of all that destruction had been burned into his brain.

Part of him wondered, as it had once before, if his deep reaction wasn't an instinctual one. The aliens had been harvesting Earth for a long time. He wondered if an antipathy toward the aliens' appearance and toward the nanoharvesters wasn't, after all this time, hardwired into the human mind.

Those were questions for the future, when the tenth

planet was streaming back to the cold dark part of its 2006-year orbit, when Cross and his team could evaluate every intriguing detail with no looming deadline.

But the deadline was swiftly approaching and he had a report to finish. He had to let Maddox—and through her, all the military leaders worldwide—know the important aspects of the alien character.

He looked longingly at the couch he had had some grad students carry into this office. The couch was the size of a twin bed and was softer than most mattresses. He'd been napping on it off and on for days now.

But he didn't have time for a nap, not even a short one. He needed to finish this report. He left his stuffy office and its tempting couch and walked toward the cafeteria.

Britt had started calling it the mess because that was what it had become. Some of the government employees who staffed it had stopped coming to work, and those who remained—mostly single people whose families lived far away—could barely make a dent in the collection of coffee cups, dirty dishes, and stained pots.

Federal sanitation regulations had gone out the window over a month ago. No one cooked for the entire group anymore. Many of the researchers simply took what they could find. Others started up the industrial strength oven or lit a burner on the stove and found themselves cooking a meal for several hungry people enticed by the smell.

The kitchen workers did try to keep the basics in stock—fresh bread, milk, some juices and fruits—but it was getting harder as the aliens' arrival got nearer. Food supplies were not moving across the nation by truck anymore. Whatever food was in a city was all that the city had. By government order, restaurants were now being used as soup kitchens to feed the growing populations.

Life as Cross had known it for the first forty-some years of his existence had vanished. In its place was a brave new world that he hadn't had time to explore, let alone understand.

The mess smelled of that badly cooked hamburger, onions, and chocolate chip cookies. One of the telescope scientists baked cookies every night to relax, or so she said. Britt theorized that the scientist did it because no one else was making sweets and in times of crisis, people craved sweets.

Cross knew that he did.

He grabbed one of the cookies and stared at the pile of dirty dishes sitting in gray water in one of the stainless steel sinks. Then he rolled up his sleeves and plunged his hands into the cold, greasy water.

He needed to do something besides stare at computer screens. Physical movement cleared his mind. Before all of this, he played racquetball, but he didn't have time for much right now. He needed to be as close to his office as possible, so that when he was ready to go back to the actual writing of the report, he could just wander there.

He pulled the dishes out of the greasy water and stacked them on the big stainless steel counter beside the sink. Once he got them out, he pulled the plug and cleaned out the sink before running fresh, hot water into it. Then he proceeded to do all the dishes by hand.

The biggest frustration he had was that no one had been able to crack the aliens' language. Experts from all over the world had been struggling with the bits of language that seemed to be written inside the downed ships. The original Tenth Planet Project was using linguists from all over the world, but in the last month, Cross had brought in several other experts: cryptologists, computer programmers, and mathematicians were the largest group, but he also brought in some music theorists and archaeologists who specialized in the ancient worlds.

When Maddox had questioned bringing in more experts, he had told her that some scientists, from the popular Carl Sagan of the last century to most of the astronomers and biologists working today, had theorized that mathematics was the universal language, and rather than let the linguists struggle with this alone, he would let others look at it from various perspectives. Musical patterns, cryptology, and ancient dialects might provide the key as easily as discovering a "word" that both cultures had in common.

So far, none of his experts had found anything, and Cross wasn't really surprised by that. Just frustrated.

Terribly frustrated.

He had made it through a mound of plates before he had to let the water out again. His hands were chapped and slime-covered. He washed them off, then bent over and tried to figure out how to work the large industrial-strength–sized dishwasher.

The problem—and it was one he had told no one—was that he wasn't certain the squiggles they had found in the alien ship were a written language. They might have been symbols that designated how the controls worked, for example, the way that international symbols worked—like the one of a person in a wheelchair that indicated handicapped access. If that was the case, he knew, even with his limited education in this area, that none of his people would crack a code. They would be baffled by this until the end of time.

He cleared the dishes out of the washer and began to stack the greasy pots and pans inside.

The other problem that he had was that he had no real sense of the aliens' culture. He knew a lot about them, given that he hadn't even known that aliens existed a year ago, but he didn't know as much as he wanted to.

He had already told Maddox a lot about the aliens, but he would formalize what he knew into the report. Some of what he had received from the other members of the Project would help in the attack. Some of it might become useful later on, in ways that Cross wasn't sure of yet.

What he did know was this: the aliens had a hierarchical society. The command center of their ships was laid out so that one creature rose above the rest. That creature had the best view of the others, and the most information on his console—based primarily on size of the unit.

He also knew that these creatures were extremely intelligent and that for hundreds of thousands of years their culture was significantly more advanced than that of humans. He suspected that they were startled to have humans attack them in space—as startled as humans would be to learn that ants had developed space travel.

That advantage was lost though; the aliens now knew that they were fighting a more advanced race than the ones they had seen two thousand years ago.

The aliens had a knowledge of tactics. The fact that they did not harvest the same area each time told him that they understood the value of planning. Several of his biologists theorized from the way the aliens changed their method of attack in the last real battle that they also had an understanding of emotions.

Retaliation, or so he was told, was not an intellectual concept. Its initial basis lay in emotion. Retaliation came from anger, and an escalated response was designed to subdue a lesser force.

Humans had not been subdued. Therefore, some of the biologists theorized, the aliens would try harder to put humans in their places and out of the way.

Cross closed the dishwasher door and started it. It whirred to life with a force that startled him. There were still countless dishes around him. But he had no interest in them any longer.

He was beginning to get a handle on his report.

But Cross knew, because he saw all of the information, and because he, too, had been studying the aliens, that what was most important to the aliens wasn't revenge or subduing Earth.

It was survival.

Everything about the aliens showed that they had to conserve. They had developed a way to survive even after they had lost their original sun. It required them to suffer long periods of darkness and, the experts hypothesized, a cold sleep that lasted centuries. It was a brilliant solution for the aliens, but it imposed strict limitations on them.

He ticked off the limitations in his mind.

—They had only a small amount of time in which to harvest all the food and energy they needed for two thousand years.

—If they could still reproduce, they had to do so in the short span of time they were near the sun.

—If they had to build or repair new things, they had to do so within that same short period of time.

Cross likened it in his mind to the way humans lived two hundred years ago, when cross-country travel was time-consuming and difficult. Those who lived in extreme northern climates spent the short summers working fields, growing food, and preparing for the long winters.

That was what the aliens were doing.

Only this time they had encountered a serious disaster, similar to a spring drought, combined with summer wildfires that had ravaged not only the fields, but the homes of the farmers as well. If aliens did not have a successful harvest this time, they would not survive their long harsh winter. They would be destroyed.

They were fighting for everything. And when *humans* had everything at stake, they made mistakes.

Cross could only hope the aliens would.

That would be the basis of his final report to Maddox. That, and one other thing. Humans, when they were pushed to the very edge, when they knew they had to prevail or they would lose everything, became extremely dangerous creatures.

Maddox and the world leaders who were trying to fight these aliens had to get them to spend too much energy, had to prevent their harvest, and had to protect themselves against an even more frightening enemy than the one Earth had first encountered.

Because, Cross suspected, the aliens were as determined—perhaps even more determined—than the humans were.

Cross believed that humans, even after all they had been through, didn't entirely understand the finality of this fight.

He also believed that the aliens knew that if they lost this fight, they would lose everything.

He was afraid that distinction would make all of the difference.

November 10, 2018
11:49 Universal Time

Second Harvest: First Day

General Gail Banks squeezed against the control panel in the newest section of the International Space Station. The remains of her crew—the best, most important members—were pressed around her, concentrating on their work inside the long, narrow control room.

In the last thirty days, she had transferred all of the ISS's operations into this space. It had taken some work. Over the years, the ISS had scattered its operations throughout the various sections. So in addition to all the work the crew was doing for the fight against the tenth planet, Banks had had to siphon off some of her better programmers to make certain operations came out of one room.

That way, she at least had a chance of saving lives.

She had evacuated nonessential personnel to the surface yesterday. The eighteen remaining knew they were on a suicide mission. All of them had had the opportunity to leave and none of them had taken it.

Banks doubted she would have offered them the opportunity to leave if she thought any of them would. She needed them to launch the missiles. It was a job she couldn't do alone.

She gazed at the small viewscreen above her. One hundred seventy-nine missiles were scattered across its surface like tiny black slashes against the universe. These missiles were not the hodgepodge she had had in the summer. Most of these had been built—quickly—for this mission.

And she hoped the aliens had no idea they were here.

There was no way of verifying what the aliens knew, of course, but the scientists on the surface said they saw no evidence of the aliens' having the abilities that so many science fictional aliens did—of scanning through planets, of using instrumentation that read through solid rock. Earth was gambling on that, and gambling hard.

In the last month, Banks had moved the space station. She had sped up its orbit slightly so that when the aliens passed the moon coming toward Earth, it would be on the far side of the Earth.

Hidden.

The nuclear-tipped missiles were hidden near the ISS. She was going to launch them at the tenth planet.

She hoped that the ISS's position would give them enough time to launch the missiles out of Earth's gravity well and on their way before the aliens saw them. If the aliens saw them, they could suck the energy out of the missiles here, and the missiles would plunge uselessly to Earth.

The key was to get the missiles heading toward the tenth planet before the aliens even knew they existed.

Banks's fingers moved across her control panel. This launching was much more difficult than the last. With the last, she had had the entire crew of the ISS. This time, she had barely what she needed.

She would have kept a few more, but this was all she could cram into a shuttle. Even though she knew their chances of getting off the ISS were slim, she was still going to try. The only people who achieved the impossible were the people who attempted the impossible.

The shuttle was standing by, waiting for her crew to finish their task and abandon the station.

The alien fleet was within the moon's orbit and heading toward Earth.

The time was now, whether she was ready or not. And she was ready.

Everything was working smoothly. She'd even had time to double-check all systems.

"General," Lief Anderssen said as he monitored the information before him. "Alien fleet is moving into orbit just as we had expected."

Banks nodded. Anderssen was a slender, balding blond whose only task had been to monitor the alien fleet. He would continue to do so, but he would also help launch the missiles.

Although Banks didn't say anything, she was relieved that the aliens were acting according to plan. The experts had been right. The aliens were extremely energy conscious, and they were coming in on the most direct and energy-efficient way to orbit the Earth.

"Two minutes and eighteen seconds to optimum launch window," said Sofia Razi. Her dark head was bent over her console, and her body was contorted as she tried to fit into her small station. Razi was taller than most assigned to the ISS, but she was the very best officer Banks had ever worked with. Banks had juggled a lot of red tape to get Razi here.

Banks glanced out the small port at the stars beyond. The hope was that the rockets could be launched while the alien ships were dropping into orbit on the far side of Earth. The missiles would move around the planet, staying out of sight of the alien ships until they left Earth's orbit, headed for a location in space where the tenth planet would be in sixteen days.

By the time the missiles were detected by the alien

112

fleet, it would be too late to both do a harvest and intercept the missiles. Banks's hope was that the aliens would protect their home world instead of doing the harvest.

Some had argued that the aliens would never leave their planet unguarded, and that the missiles were a waste of time and resources. But others had argued strongly that the aliens were so energy conservative, and so focused on getting what they needed from Earth for the coming cold sleep, that every ship would be sent in the fleet to Earth, leaving the tenth planet unguarded.

That idea went against everything Banks had ever learned in the military. But the fundamental idea made sense, and as the president had said, it was worth the gamble.

So she and seventeen others were willing to give their lives for this crazy idea, just in case it stopped the coming attack.

"One minute."

Banks moved her fingers along her console, monitoring the same information her staff was giving her. She had only one hands-on duty, and that would come last. The rest of her duties were all in making certain everything went according to plan.

The long narrow room was stuffy. The environmental controls had not been monitored in nearly twenty-four hours, and somewhere along the way, they had left their normal mark. Or perhaps it was just the tension in the room. The entire crew knew they probably wouldn't make it off the ISS alive.

They had to make certain the missiles launched, and launched properly, or they would all die for nothing.

"Thirty seconds."

She waited, not allowing herself to hold her breath.

On the screen the missiles were cold, dark streaks against the blackness of space.

"Time," Razi finally said.

"Launch," Banks ordered.

In the blackness of space 179 missiles, every rocket and warhead the human race could get into space in the short time allowed, fired.

Banks watched through the port. The blackness around their small section of the ISS vanished, burned away in the brightness of the large launch. Then she glanced at her viewscreen. The imagery she had just seen was repeated on a tiny scale.

Silence filled the control room. Banks held her breath.

Seconds ticked by.

"All fired," Razi said. "All on course."

"Yeah!" Anderssen cheered like a boy, but he was the only one.

They didn't have time to gloat. Not if they wanted to live.

"Transfer all telemetry to ground stations," Banks said.

"Transferred," Razi said.

With one last look at the rockets firing, now just faint dots of light hovering like a group of fireflies over the edge of Earth below, she turned to her crew.

"Let's get the hell out of here," she said.

They had exactly eighteen minutes to abandon the station and drop the shuttle out of orbit before the alien spacecraft would be on top of them. If the aliens were true to form, they'd drain the energy from this place. If Banks and her crew stayed, they would die here. Their air would run out first or they'd freeze to death.

She wasn't going to die that way.

None of them were.

Making sure everyone was ahead of her, she gave one quick glance around the control room, then reached down and keyed in one last command.

The computers would track the incoming alien ships. When they were almost close enough to drain the energy from the station, it would explode with enough hydrogen bombs to level half of Europe.

The ISS had become just another weapon in the many that Earth would be throwing at the aliens this time. But if the ISS took out even one alien ship, it would be worth it.

Quickly she headed behind her crew toward the shuttle. Twelve minutes to board, release from the station, and drop into the atmosphere. No one had ever done that in under an hour before.

But they would.

They had to.

They had no other choice except death.

5

November 10, 2018
2:37 A.M. Central Standard Time

Second Harvest: First Day

Kara sat on the ruined kitchen stool, the one crazed Denny Zefio had sliced with his pocketknife. The beautiful leather top had been pulled together with packer's tape, but it wasn't as comfortable as it used to be.

Nothing was.

Kara leaned her head against the living room wall. Half the boarders were in here, watching the screens. The other half were in their rooms, pretending to sleep. Kara's mother was making the next day's bread as if nothing were happening. The entire house smelled of yeast and dough.

Her mother's solution to this entire crisis seemed to be a personality transformation. She was trying to be the perfect homemaker. Now that she didn't have to report to work—no one had to go to nonessential jobs—

she tried to make sure everyone was comfortable, and that was proving to be quite a task.

Especially when she didn't trust most of them.

Her mother had removed all of the important, heirloomy stuff and boxed it before the stool incident, even before she had found out that she would have strangers in her home as well as family. She had started packing away all the "good" stuff the day that Kara had arrived home from her trek downtown, the day her father said she shouldn't refer to if she didn't want to upset her mother.

Kara had thought her mother was too preoccupied with saving all the valuables to notice anything, though she had welcomed her home with a big hug and kiss, and had expressed a lot of worry.

But ever since, when Kara started to leave the house, her mother always demanded to know where she was going.

Her father said that was how her mother showed she cared. Kara would have liked a little less caring and a little more freedom, especially now that the house was stuffed like a square sausage.

It didn't even look like her house anymore. Her family's furniture had been pushed against the wall and covered with blankets to make more room. Other people—the "guests," as her mother called them, as if they had been invited instead of mandated—had brought some furniture of their own, mostly comfortable chairs, although one elderly woman had brought a bed that could fold into half a hundred different positions and had to be plugged into the wall.

Only the elaborate TV setup remained the same, and now all the screens were on all the time. After a few days, her father had found headphones for each screen, and unless everyone in the living room had agreed on a station, the viewer was required to wear them.

Her father had become what Kara privately called Ruler of the House. He set forth rules like proclamations, threatening anyone who didn't comply with eviction. And everyone knew he would do it, too. He had evicted crazy Denny Zefio and his family—and when they had appealed the decision to the local FEMA office, her father had gone into full lawyer mode, bringing in other members of the household as witnesses as to why the Zefios were too dangerous to be sheltered with "normal" people.

Kara didn't think any of these people were normal.

Her cousins from Beloit had insisted on bringing their two dachshunds, both of which were puppies and neither of which were trained. Her grandparents, from Joliet, had brought her grandmother's entire spoon collection and wanted to display it on the kitchen wall— her mother had agreed, probably hoping the ugly thing would be stolen. Her father's best friend from grade school had brought his third wife and her four children, none of whom got along.

And those were the people that Kara had known before all this began. The strangers were living up to that name, as well.

The house was big, so they were required to take in several families. And that didn't count the people who had pitched tents on the lawn. Her mother's roses were forever ruined, or so she said. Her father just rolled his eyes; he, like Kara, knew there was a good chance that the roses wouldn't bloom again anyway.

The strangers included Barb, the elderly woman; crazy Denny and his family; their replacements, the Nelsons; and the Hendricksons, whose son, Connor, was just a little too cute to be ignored.

Kara now shared her room with her cousins Eve and Michelle, and could barely stand to go in there. It smelled of cheap perfume most of the time, and there was no longer a floor to walk on. Mostly, she had to step over piles of clothes—some of which were hers, because Eve had no notion of asking before she put something on.

Kara had complained to her father just once, and he had looked at her with that measuring gaze he sometimes had. *If you can think of something better*, he had said, *do it. Otherwise, why don't you look at all the other houses around here? Everyone's going through the same thing.*

Not quite everyone.

Old Mr. McMasters down the street got busted for charging his "guests" for everything from parking to food. He was told to stop or move out of his own house.

The Stanhopes had gotten some kind of exemption, claiming too many family members, but Kara had never seen anyone but the two of them. For a while, she had thought they were going to get away with it, but as the neighborhood caught on, more and more of the tent people moved into the Stanhopes' yard. They may have had the inside of the house all to themselves, but they couldn't cross the yard anymore. And they didn't get city-sponsored rations because they couldn't provide evidence of boarders.

The food was turning out to be more important than anyone thought. Kara's mother and Barb spent a lot of their time online, filling out the forms that gave them permission for their rations. Barb was training the others to fill out the paper forms, as well. She was afraid that the power would go out, and then there would be no computers at all.

Kara couldn't imagine a world like that. She couldn't imagine a world without electricity, even though she'd been through one outage, in that awful blizzard of '15. Nothing had worked then, and she had been afraid she was going to die.

Only she hadn't known then how fear really felt.

She did now.

The aliens were supposed to come back tonight. She had tried to go to bed, but there was no sleeping, not with Michelle's snoring, and Eve's whimpering bad dreams. Kara had lain on her back in her bed—at least she still had her bed—arms folded behind her head, and stared at the ceiling, wishing she could see through it to the sky.

She knew, she just knew, the aliens were going to try to destroy Chicago. And she had a hunch they'd miss and hit Lake Forest. She and her family had had too much luck already. Yeah, they had lost the other set of cousins out west, but they hadn't really been touched otherwise. Even the president's declaration that only areas within a twenty-mile radius of a major city center would be protected hadn't affected them in the way she had thought. Lake Forest was theoretically outside the protection zone, but since half of that zone was Lake Michigan, the FEMA people and the city governments decided to spread their safety zones north along the lakefront.

People south of the city were screaming discrimination, but they didn't have any recourse. They had to move north. There wasn't time to sue or to fight anything in the courts.

Or, as Kara's father said, they could just stay home and take their chances.

Almost no one wanted to do that.

So they were all coming north. Kara's once quiet neighborhood was a sea of tents and cars and strangers. There was no place to have privacy anymore. She couldn't go to her room and she couldn't go outside. Even if she went to the park, she would find tents filled with people, most of whom were snarling at each other because they never got a moment's peace.

And things got even tenser yesterday when the planes flew over. They dropped grayish black stuff from the skies and everyone got scared, as if the aliens had come with planes instead of big huge spaceships.

Kara had pretended not to be scared—she'd heard the warnings that this was going to happen, same as everyone else—but her heart pounded hard all the same.

The powder, which up close was more gray than black, covered everything. The whole area had been sprayed several times, and no one could walk across the street without leaving footprints.

After the second spraying, Kara had gone outside and crouched, trying to see the nanorescuers up close. She had seen the video of the rescuers eating the alien machines. That had impressed her dad, but she hadn't understood how there would be enough rescuers. How had the government known how many rescuers to make? Had they counted all the ones the aliens had sent down before? Kara couldn't imagine how they would have been able to do that: the aliens had sucked most of them back up again.

So she figured the government was guessing, and if they guessed wrong, everyone would die.

But she didn't say anything about her suspicions to anyone, not her father, not her stupid cousins, not even Barb who seemed—despite her folding bed—like one of the most sensible people in the house. Kara had just crouched and tried to study the rescuers, and she hadn't really seen a thing.

They didn't even move. She had at least expected them to move. But they lay like sand on the pavement, shifting only when a wind blew them around.

Now, on the screens, commentators were talking nervously about the aliens' return. Some were showing simulated views from orbit—none of the stations had any way of filming above the Earth. All of their equipment had been confiscated for use by the governments, something that relieved Kara, but seemed to be annoying the commentators.

And the Nelsons and the Hendricksons—except for

Connor—had been trying to find out what was going on all day. Connor was in his room, which used to be the guest room, pretending to sleep. No one who was sensible would sleep tonight.

The world might end tonight. How could you sleep through it?

Kara pushed away from the wall and jumped off the stool. All these people were too close. She wondered where her father was. Probably in his study, since the Nelsons, who slept there, were out here. He hated that anyone had use of his study, but he didn't say anything. He believed everyone had to do his duty and not complain.

Well, Kara wasn't complaining either, except to herself. She grabbed her coat off the rack and opened the door.

"Who's that?" her mother shouted from the kitchen, but no one answered her. Kara quietly closed the door behind her and stepped onto the porch.

The air was cold and crystal clear. It felt like snow, and looked, with the nanorescuers on the ground, as if it already had. Kara looked up, but saw only light in the night sky. There were too many artificial lights in the Chicago area to allow her to see the stars.

Then she stepped off the porch and onto the sidewalk. The tents were zipped up for the night. She felt sorry for the people inside. The tents, even with their built in thermal units, had to be cold and cramped. Her father had said that, if she really looked, she could see people who were worse off than they were.

She hadn't really realized that all she had to do was look outside her front door.

The street wasn't empty, though, as she had been expecting. Some of her neighbors had pulled their lawn chairs out of winter storage and placed them on the asphalt. Others were standing nearby, hands buried in their armpits as they tried to keep warm.

Everyone was looking up, and no one was saying anything.

That was why she hadn't noticed all the people at first. It was so very quiet. The dozens of people in the street should have been making some kind of noise.

But she wasn't either. She couldn't even bring herself to say hello to them. The cold air made her feel as if she were encased in a sheet of ice, separating her from the world.

She went to the curb and looked up again. Still no stars. She wouldn't be able to see the alien ship until it was right overhead. And then it would be too late.

Maybe she would see it as a darkness, a flat darkness, above her. Maybe it would block out the lights of the city or reflect the streetlights from below.

Or maybe it would be nothing at all, as silent as the people around her, and barely visible.

She had only her imagination as her guide on this. Her imagination and all that news footage she had seen last spring.

She shuddered, and drew her coat in closer. Mrs. Lauderdale from across the street had a blanket wrapped around her, and she wore a knit cap on her gray hair. She was leaning back in her deck chair, her mouth slightly open, as if she were trying to catch candy being tossed from a balcony.

Why did Mrs. Lauderdale think she was safer out here? If those alien harvesters fell from the sky right now, they would land in her mouth and chew her up from the inside out—rescuers or no rescuers. The rescuers attacked the harvesters after they landed, jumped on them like bugs, and sucked all the energy out of them. They couldn't do that to any harvester inside someone.

Kara shuddered and glanced at her house. The roof was darker, coated with a light dusting of the grayish rescuers. They would stop anything that landed on the house. They would protect the people inside.

The people outside were taking an awful chance. They had to know it. Why weren't they acting on it?

Why wasn't she?

She shuddered one more time and went back up the sidewalk. Better to be inside with her snoring cousins or the annoying Nelsons than it was to be out here, where the harvesters could touch her before the rescuers could help.

Her father would probably say that she was being foolish. But her father—one of the most sensible people she'd ever known—was inside.

Kara went inside, too, walking past the vid screens with their useless information to the kitchen where her mother was making the final loaf of bread.

The flour, spread on the counter, looked like bleached nanorescuers.

"Do we still have sugar, Mom?" Kara asked.

Her mother looked up, a dot of flour on her nose. "I think so."

"Can we make something with it? Something good?"

Her mother smiled. It was a tired, yet understanding smile. "I don't see why not," her mother said.

And together they hauled out her great-grandmother's baking book, and looked for something good. Something sinful. Something that would make them feel as if the world weren't going to end today.

November 10, 2018
4:03 A.M. Eastern Standard Time

Second Harvest: First Day

Doug Mickelson paced the length of the Map Room and silently cursed the fact there was only one window. That window overlooked an outdoor walkway that, if memory served him right, was built over 150 years before to ease the flow of visitors out of the White House.

There was no flow of visitors into or out of the White House these days. The White House had been declared off limits to the general public, not that Mickelson could believe anyone would want to tour the place. The tensions in the nation, in the entire world, were so high that people were thinking only of survival, not of their nation's history.

He had his hands clasped. He did so to prevent his fingers from finding the edge of the curtain and pulling it back. He was in the Map Room, with the president and six other trusted friends and advisers, precisely because it had one window and could be easily guarded.

The president was seen as the center of the entire worldwide defense against the aliens. Because he had made the rallying speeches, he was the focal point, and because there were still a handful of crazies who believed that the aliens' return was just a plot, created by the government, the Secret Service and the FBI believed the president had to take as many precautions as possible.

Mickelson believed it, too. He was just feeling claustrophobic. Tonight he wanted to be outside, looking at the sky.

The president was restless, too. He was standing in front of the fireplace, warming his hands over it as if he had a permanent chill. Beside him stood Shamus O'Grady, the president's national security adviser, and on the other side was Tavi Bernstein, head of the FBI.

Grace Lopez, the chief of staff, sat in one of the antique, upholstered chairs. Carlton Hagen, one of the president's personal aides, sat beside Lopez, and the first lady, who had served as Franklin's closest adviser from the moment of their marriage, stood near the embroidered fire screen.

Patrick Aldrich, the press secretary, had been going in and out, attempting to control the flow of information, trying to prevent an international panic.

Someone—Mickelson didn't know who, but he sus-

pected it was someone on Cross's Tenth Planet team—
had predicted the aliens' return down to the second.
Cross, whom Mickelson had been friends with since
childhood, had sworn that the aliens would be predictable, and so far they had been. According to the
last report the president had gotten, the aliens were
going to arrive in Earth's orbit exactly at the moment
they had been predicted to.

Which was right about now.

Mickelson moved away from the window and
walked the length of the room again. He was still concerned with history. He had thought it appropriate that
they were here—the Map Room had been the situation
room for Franklin Delano Roosevelt and his staff in
World War II. They had sealed off the room, not allowed entrance from anywhere except the corridor—
not even from the diplomatic reception room next
door—and posted a guard in that corridor.

Mickelson had noted the historic parallels to
Franklin—two presidents with the name Franklin, two
wars on which the survival of the world depended, and
the use of this room as a central place from which it
was all staged. Only now they had electronic equipment against the far wall, enough communications devices to keep the entire world informed five times over,
and several large screens that were currently shut off.

Franklin had grinned at Mickelson when he'd mentioned the parallels. "The White House is old enough
now, Doug, that we can find parallels for anything."

"What do you mean, sir?"

"Well, you chose to see a great war being fought

129

from this room. I see a room filled with personal defeats. This was the place where President William Jefferson Clinton gave the famous August seventeenth speech that nearly brought down his presidency."

"You don't think your presidency will end here," Mickelson had said, shocked.

Franklin's grin had faded. "I don't think so. I think the truth of this room is that it is being used as it was intended to be used, as a way station, a place to relax outside of the function of the diplomacy that was usually going on next door."

"There is no diplomacy tonight."

"War is diplomacy of a different sort."

"I was raised to believe that war was the failure of diplomacy."

Franklin had nodded. "It is. How can you have diplomacy with a group whose culture you do not understand and whose language you have never heard?"

And that was when Franklin had turned to the fire.

The first lady, a slender silver-haired woman who had given up her place as CEO of a major corporation to accompany her husband to the White House, had looked at Mickelson then. In her intelligent brown eyes, Mickelson saw both reproach and understanding.

Now she had her right hand on her husband's back. "Thayer," she said softly, "this room is not comfortable. Perhaps we should do as the Joint Chiefs asked and use the war room in the basement."

The basement was a euphemistic term for the bunkers that had been built below the White House. The first set had been built during the Cold War of the previous century. The current set, shown to the president and his cabinet on their first day in office, was the fourth incarnation of the same plan. Only this one had been modernized during the presidency of Franklin's predecessor. The bunkers actually made Mickelson feel as if he had stepped into the middle of someone's paranoid fantasies.

In addition to all the working rooms, from conference rooms to offices to situation rooms complete with their own electrical grid, there were apartments for the various governmental officials and their spouses, several kitchens—stocked with enough food to last years—and a defensive system that should withstand any kind of bombardment save total destruction of the Earth itself.

Mickelson hated the bunkers worse than he hated being in the Map Room. To go to the basement seemed to him as if they were conceding that the aliens were going to win the war.

Franklin turned to his wife, but as he was about to answer, his beeper went off. Mickelson stiffened. He knew what that meant—they all knew what it meant—but Franklin checked his wrist'puter anyway.

"The aliens have entered Earth's orbit," he said.

For a moment, everyone in the room froze. Mickelson knew that if he lived through this attack, he would remember that sentence forever. And the somber tone Franklin used to express it.

O'Grady turned on the screens. Most of them showed the video pictures from the telescopes. One hundred eight alien ships, looking like black shadows against the Earth. One hundred eight, all with the capability to destroy everything.

"Have those ships seen the missiles yet?" Franklin asked.

No one answered. Everyone in the room knew as much as he did.

"Have they?"

"Sir, there's no way of telling from here," said Grace Lopez. She hadn't moved from her chair.

"Then someone go find out!" Franklin snapped.

O'Grady headed toward the door. He glanced one last time at the screens as he did so, as if he saw his own death depicted there. And then he disappeared into the corridor.

Mickelson gripped his hands tightly together. The missiles had left Earth's orbit, and in a few minutes, the alien ships would see them. If the aliens didn't take the bait and go after the missiles, the missiles would hit the tenth planet in sixteen days.

Sixteen days for one attack. This was the slowest moving war in Earth's entire history.

O'Grady returned a moment later. Yolanda Hayes, the science adviser, was with him.

Mickelson was startled at her appearance. He hadn't seen Hayes since the night he introduced her to Leo Cross, about a year ago. Then she had been stylish, made-up, and manicured, her hair cut in the latest style. Now, she wore no makeup at all, her nails were ragged, and her dress was rumpled. Her hair needed a cut, as well.

It wasn't that she seemed depressed. Just distracted.

"Mr. President," she said.

"Yolanda." Franklin hadn't turned his attention from the screens. "Do those ships know about the missiles?"

"Not yet, sir," she said. "They will shortly. They can't quite see them yet. We don't know if they have the right equipment to detect them without a visual."

Mickelson bit his lower lip. If they had already detected the missiles, then they weren't responding. Having the missiles hit the tenth planet wasn't the defense they were all hoping for.

Those ships had to leave Earth's orbit.

All of them, preferably.

"I got word that General Banks and her crew got off the International Space Station," Hayes said. "They're on the *Endeavor II*."

Franklin nodded. Mickelson took a deep breath and held it for just a moment. Banks and her crew had done a fantastic job launching the missiles. All of the senior White House staff had been notified of this suicide mission. No one expected Banks or the crew to get off the ISS. The fact that they had managed it was nothing short of a miracle.

But, he knew, they needed more than one miracle to get them to Earth in one piece.

"Where is the *Endeavor II?*" Franklin asked.

"At last report," Hayes said, "still attached to the ISS. But the fact that the crew is in the shuttle means that it'll leave any minute now. It probably already has."

Mickelson hoped so. They were running out of time. He glanced at the screens. The shadow ships seemed darker somehow. More ominous.

He couldn't concentrate on Banks and her crew. He had to think about the rest of the world. If those ships didn't follow the missiles, then the first part of the plan had failed.

"I hope to hell this works," Franklin said. "How soon will we know if they take the bait?"

"They'll have to respond within the hour, sir," Hayes said. "And once they commit ships to chasing the missiles, those ships will not be able to return to Earth."

"Once they commit?" Franklin said. "You're that certain that they will?"

"Yessir," Hayes said without missing a beat.

Mickelson remembered the meeting where this plan was drawn up. Franklin had asked the same question then. But, like Mickelson, he had probably thought that the aliens would see the missiles and then follow them immediately. Neither of them had expected this delay.

"The laws of physics are on our side, sir," Hayes said.

"I'm glad something is," Franklin muttered.

Mickelson's 'puter vibrated against his wrist. He looked down, saw that he had an important call, and pressed a button to transfer it to his personal pocket phone so that the entire room didn't have to hear the whole conversation.

He took the phone out of his pocket, flipped it open, turned his back on the group, and answered. One of his most trusted deputies gave him the quick code. Mickelson thanked him and hung up.

Franklin was still clarifying details with Hayes.

"Excuse me, sir," Mickelson said. "That was my European team. The last of the major cities have been protected."

"That was too close for comfort," Franklin said. "Someone want to tell me again why Europe was the last to be covered?"

"It was the second run," Mickelson said, and then wished he hadn't. Franklin knew that. He was just getting edgy and wanted someone to take it out on.

"It was too close," Franklin said. "It's all been too close. Finishing our cities six hours ago was too close."

"The factories are still running at full capacity, sir," Hayes said. "We're going to cover as much as we can even with the aliens overhead. We're not going to stop unless they stop us."

"I know that, Yolanda," Franklin said. "I just want some movement. That's all. I want those aliens to leave orbit. And I want it now."

He hadn't raised his voice, but the effect was the same. No one else in the room spoke. The first lady hadn't moved away from the fireplace. She was watching her husband with a mixture of bemusement and concern.

"Is this the slowest damn war in the history of the planet? Or am I just impatient?" Franklin asked.

"We're covering great distances, sir," Hayes said. "We can't expect—"

"I suspect the Roman conquest seemed a lot more protracted," Mickelson said, knowing that history could sometimes distract Franklin. "Imagine having to

135

cover the same sort of great distance with primitive equipment—and not having instant communication."

Franklin glared at him. "I hate it when you do that, Doug." And then he smiled, although it was a distracted smile.

Aldrich entered the room, glanced at the screens, and then stopped in front of Franklin. "Sir—"

"Tell me that the ships have left Earth's orbit."

"I could, sir, but it wouldn't be the truth."

Franklin shook his head. Then he glanced at Mickelson. "All right. What were you going to report?"

"Just that we got a final update on the state of the population, now that they know the aliens have entered orbit."

"Wonderful," Franklin said. "Let me guess. They're scared and beginning to riot."

"No, sir," Aldrich said. "No rioting. In fact, they're remarkably calm."

"That's a tribute to you, dear," the first lady said.

Franklin rolled his eyes. "Don't suck up to me now, Cara."

"I never have, Thayer." She spoke softly.

He turned toward her and the look that passed between them made Mickelson jealous. He'd never had anyone look at him with such perfect understanding.

Aldrich waited a moment before adding, "The last of the military and the police are being pulled back from the rural areas and the small towns. The cities, even though they're crowded, are extremely silent."

"Seems almost unnatural," Killius said.

"All of this is unnatural," Mickelson said. He would

have put money on more disturbances in the cities, or the largest new city—the camp out in Death Valley. Hundreds of thousands of people opted to camp there, afraid, apparently of the nanorescuers and the government control. They had formed their own control, filled with survivalists and gun nuts, but it seemed to be working for them.

Tavi Bernstein had said earlier that she believed the city in Death Valley would remain a city if the world survived.

Mickelson looked at Bernstein now. She hadn't left her place beside the fireplace. She was watching the screens with a calmness that seemed false. He went to her side, wanting to put his arm around her, but knowing that wouldn't be appropriate.

She looked up at him. "Somehow I never really believed they'd come back."

Propriety be damned. He put his arm around her and pulled her close. Her small body was rigid, but it slowly relaxed into him.

He had believed the aliens would come back. He had believed it so deep down that their appearance was almost anticlimactic. He just wanted to get through the next few days, to receive the answer to the question he'd been harboring since he understood what the aliens were doing.

He wanted to know if the human race would survive.

"We're as ready as we can be for them," he said to her.

"I know that." Her voice was soft. Tavi's reputation was built on her toughness. The fact that she let him touch her, that she revealed a soft side at all, showed how deeply worried she was about all of this.

"Thayer," the first lady said again. "We'd be getting better updates in the basement."

Franklin's lips thinned, but the fondness he had shown her earlier remained in his eyes. "I hate it when you're right, Cara," he said.

Then he paused. For a moment, Mickelson thought Franklin would keep them in the Map Room.

Franklin's gaze turned toward Mickelson. "I guess it's time to go to a new room, where we make our own history."

Mickelson nodded. He didn't want to go to the basement, but he knew the move was inevitable. And the time was now, while they were waiting.

He hated waiting. But, he knew, it would be over soon.

November 10, 2018
4:19 A.M. Eastern Standard Time

Second Harvest: First Day

The aliens were in Earth's orbit and General Maddox no longer had time to read reports. So, even though more information kept pouring through Cross's links, he had left his office. He was in Britt's lab, sitting on a desk toward the back, trying to stay out of the way.

It was impossible to tell it was the middle of the

night. The entire staff was there, working intently. Britt, her hair sticking up in spikes, was bent over a screen, discussing the telemetry with one of her assistants.

Cross managed a lot of information, both in his own career and for the Tenth Planet Project, but he had no idea how Britt did it. In this massive room, on hundreds of screens, not to mention the large wall screen at the base of the room, the scientists monitored the telemetry and images from a dozen different sources. And that didn't count the space telescopes, which were sending their own information back to this lab.

From his vantage, Cross could see the video from two cameras that were tracking the missiles headed out of Earth's orbit. The entire room had stopped working to watch the launch. The air had been tense with excitement and nerves. Once the missiles launched, however, everything went back to normal—heads bent over desks, conversations ceasing, the hum of machines and the occasional beep from a screen the only sounds in the room.

Sometimes someone would make a verbal report, but the amount of response it got made it sound as if that person had been talking to himself.

Cross also knew that a dozen orbiting satellites were tracking the alien ships as they swung into a wide orbit around Earth. The ships were using gravity to slow themselves down. Cross had watched the alien ships on one of the scopes for a little while, then realized that just seeing them increased the knot in his stomach, so he stopped.

Not that he could do anything anyway. He was just watching, as were most of the people in the lab. The Army had dozens of satellites of their own, as did other countries, but still Britt and her people were forwarding all their images to twenty different headquarters around the world, as well as to General Maddox's headquarters.

Ever since the missiles flared away from Earth, the view Cross studied came from a camera attached to the International Space Station. General Gail Banks, a hard-as-nails military type, had captured his attention during his brief meeting with her months ago. He had been impressed with her then, and that feeling had grown the more he learned about her.

When he realized she had taken on a suicide mission to save the Earth, he had found his attention focused on her more and more. In some ways, he felt responsible for her. If he hadn't discovered the tenth planet before it arrived, she wouldn't be there now.

Of course, if he hadn't found it then, the Earth wouldn't be able to defend itself. He knew that. Understanding didn't stop his interest in the general.

At the moment, the ISS camera was trained on the shuttle, the *Endeavor II*. Small thruster jets were shoving the shuttle away from the station, seemingly far, far too slowly.

"Five minutes and eight seconds until the alien ships are at the station in their current orbit. They'll come up on it fast!"

Cross glanced over. Odette Roosevelt, one of Britt's

assistants, was apparently monitoring the shuttle as well. She was the one who had spoken.

Other scientists surreptitiously glanced at the live video coming to them from the ISS.

"They're coming damn fast," a scientist down front said.

Everyone was interested in Banks. Cross hadn't realized it. Maybe they were all afraid that Banks and her crew would be the first casualties in this new battle.

He gripped the edge of the desk, watching the thrusters continue to ignite. He had no idea what the aliens would do when they reached the ISS. If the shuttle was still there, would they know it was a ship?

He hoped not.

Britt came up to him and leaned against the desk beside him. He felt the heat from her body. She glanced at him, looking tired and worried at the same time.

The aliens had a number of options when they reached the station. Cross just wasn't sure which one they'd choose. He didn't know if they would drain the power from the station or if they would attempt to destroy it.

And the shuttle, well, draining the power from the shuttle would destroy it as completely as blowing it up. The shuttle's orbit would decay and it would fall into the atmosphere, burning up on reentry.

"They've got to make it," Odette Roosevelt said.

Cross felt that way, too. It was as if whatever happened to the shuttle crew would set the tone for what happened on Earth. He knew that was silly and super-stitious. He knew he would fight to save the Earth no matter what happened to Gail Banks.

But he wanted this one to be clean.

He wanted everyone to survive.

Britt took his hand.

He glanced at her. Her smile was sad.

They both knew that winning the war without casualties was going to be impossible.

And more than likely, General Gail Banks was going to be the first of millions.

6

November 10, 2018
9:23 Universal Time

Second Harvest: First Day

General Gail Banks had replaced the pilot at the controls of the *Endeavor II*. She was the best pilot she knew; she couldn't bear to let anyone else handle the controls—not on such a delicate mission.

She sat in the pilot's seat beside Sofia Razi, her copilot. The *Endeavor II*'s pilot, Captain Michael Thorne, was good. He had volunteered for this mission, but he didn't have as many hours beneath him piloting a shuttle as Razi or Banks had.

He sat behind Banks at her request, careful to keep an eye on her work, but she had instructed him not to say anything until they were away from the ISS. She was going to break every rule of piloting as she got the shuttle away from the station—and if her piloting caused them to fail, well, then so be it.

At least she had tried.

Through the triple-edged plastic of the pilot's windows she could see the ISS before her. She had fallen in love with that crazy jigsaw of a place. She would miss it—or, at least, she hoped she would miss it.

Right now, she was just trying to escape from it.

The lights from the overhead controls were reflecting on her board. She had always noticed that inside the docking clamps at the ISS, light reflected oddly off the white station's sides. Now the lights were distracting her, warning a part of her brain that she wasn't following protocol.

She didn't have time for protocol. She gave Razi several terse commands, and Razi's nimble hands manipulated the thrusters. Banks handled the controls. She swung the nose of the shuttle away from the ISS. The steering thrusters gave her power, but not as much as she wanted.

These shuttles were not built for speed. They never had been. They were designed for cautious missions, created in the days when going to space was an expensive rarity.

What she wished for right now was a machine with the speed and finesse of a fighter plane.

Not that that would have been practical. Not in space. In space hurrying usually meant accidents and death.

Now, not hurrying meant death.

But the shuttle's nose steering thrusters just weren't powerful enough to do anything but nudge the shuttle's large mass slowly sideways.

"One minute, thirty seconds," Ground Control said.

Razi snorted through her nose. She had wanted to shut off the tinny male voice of Ground Control, which was counting down the minutes until the aliens would be flashing into the range of the ISS.

Banks wanted GC's help. She needed it. She wanted to be in touch with a voice from the ground—and she wanted to *hear* how close the enemy was.

She knew they were too close.

The aliens were coming up so fast that there would be no visual sighting until the last few seconds. If the aliens acted true to form, they would suck the active energy out of the station and the shuttle. If she didn't get the shuttle away from the station and into the correct position to hit the atmosphere by the time they did that, the shuttle would burn up on reentry.

So far, the aliens had been predictable. She hoped they would continue to be so. Otherwise, they'd probably blow the shuttle to pieces—and Banks could do nothing about it. No one had ever expected an attack from space, and, therefore, the shuttle had no weapons.

What she wouldn't give for a weapon or two.

She made herself glance at the instrument panel and check the readings. Normal. So far so good, considering how hard she was pushing this giant hunk of a ship.

"One minute, fifteen seconds." The voice from GC sounded very far away. Banks wanted to reach out and hang onto it, as if the voice alone could pull her down to Earth.

She looked at her instrument panel again, then at the white walls of the ISS moving as the shuttle eased away from it. What no one else on the shuttle knew was that the station had been rigged with atomic warheads, ready to blow when an alien ship got within range. It looked as if the explosion would happen in about one minute. That explosion would also destroy the shuttle if it was too close.

She had known this was a suicide mission, but dammit! she wasn't ready to die.

Not yet.

The nose of the shuttle eased to the left so that it pointed beside the station and out over the curve of the Earth. The station was now out of direct line.

Barely, but enough.

"Starting main thrusters," she said, her fingers running through the sequence faster than she had ever done it before. She had barely enough room to do this—according to protocol, *Endeavor II* was still too close to the station.

The force shoved her back into her seat as the thrusters kicked on.

"Forty-five seconds," GC said, not commenting on her action.

She got the nose of the shuttle aimed at the horizon of the Earth. She could see the lights of the East Coast in darkness ahead of them.

"Still too high," Razi said.

"Thirty seconds." GC spoke as if the very words could make the shuttle move faster.

The thrust kept her shoved into her seat. Moving her fingers was difficult, but at least the motion felt familiar. Banks eased the nose of the shuttle down a little more toward the planet below.

"One kilometer from the station and accelerating," Razi said.

"Fifteen seconds." GC sounded like a damn computer. Was he as hyped up as she was? Or was he concentrating on the alien ships only, so that he wouldn't have to know if the shuttle failed to get far enough away.

"Two kilometers," Razi said. Her voice was flat, too.

Banks's heart was pounding. It seemed as if everyone on the shuttle—her entire crew—could hear it.

"Three," Razi said. This time, Banks heard a thread of hope.

She felt that same thread of hope. The farther they got away, the better.

"Four."

They were almost outside the immediate blast radius. Banks did a quick glance at everything. They were in the best position she could have hoped for under the circumstances.

"Shutting down thrusters," she said, as her fingers cut the interior back to weightlessness. Her body jumped against her safety harness. "No point in giving the aliens a flare to go by."

As she said that a large number of black dots seemed to form off to their right and above their orbit.

"Shut your eyes and put your hands over them!" Banks shouted to all the passengers. "Now! Everyone, that's an order. Atomic explosion!"

Then, seemingly instantly, their ship went black. Every instrument, every light shut down. The aliens had sucked the energy from the shuttle.

She had expected that, but it startled her nonetheless.

She ducked her head and covered her eyes, pressing her face into the soft fabric of her clothing. She hadn't had time to put on a space suit, and suddenly she regretted it.

An instant later the International Space Station exploded in a blinding white light that Gail could see even with her eyes shut and pressed into her arm. It was as if someone had shined a bright, white light into the inside of her head.

"Clear," she shouted, opening her eyes and trying to get them to adjust quickly.

Around her the shuttle's systems were completely dead.

There was no sign of the alien ships. It was as if nothing had even happened. Unlike on Earth, an explosion in space has no sound or shock wave.

And best of all, the shuttle hadn't gotten smashed by any debris—and it would have by now.

She let out a small sigh of relief. They had survived the explosion of the station.

She just hoped the alien ships hadn't been so lucky.

She took a deep breath and forced herself to think. She had managed to get the shuttle into a reentry position, but she had no idea when reentry would happen.

Her sense of time had completely disappeared.

She missed the tinny voice of Ground Control.

She glanced at Razi, who was blinking, but all right. "Any memory of how long until we hit the atmosphere?"

"Twenty minutes, give or take a few. At this speed, we'll most likely bounce once or twice before staying in."

She nodded. "Well, in twenty minutes, we're going to be damn cold. Make sure everyone is all right and get them bundled up and huddling together as best they can. But tell them that at the first bump, to get back to seats and buckle in."

"You think we might be able to dead-stick this in?"

"The rudder hydraulics in this were installed just for this contingency. They are completely pressure run, with no electricity or electronics needed. So I can at least steer when we get into some atmosphere."

"Yeah, but to where?"

Banks shot a glance at Razi. Beads of sweat covered Razi's delicate features. Banks wasn't going to let nervousness take her. Instead, she'd let the anger she felt at the damn aliens, who had stolen their energy, fuel her reentry. She had learned in Top Gun school to handle an emergency one item at a time. She brought that training to bear now.

"Good question," she said to Razi. "Let's first see if we can hit the atmosphere flat enough to not tumble and burn. Then we'll worry about where and if we can land."

Razi nodded and glanced back at the dead instruments. They both knew that without computers, they were going to come in hard and fast and who knew where.

Razi unbuckled and floated back to get the passengers secure as Banks sat, wishing for a radio, wishing for controls, wishing to be just about anywhere than in the world's heaviest glider trying to make a reentry into an atmosphere.

The aliens hadn't killed them. But physics and the laws of nature soon just might.

November 10, 2018
9:35 Universal Time

Second Harvest: First Day

Cicoi's lower tentacles were wrapped around his command circle so hard that they were going numb. His first and second eyestalks ached, and he'd had to pocket them. The others had been pocketed when the large station in the third planet's orbit had exploded, and yet he had still seen the white blast through the pockets' membranes.

He had not been blinded but his Third had. His Third had had all eyestalks extended when the explosion hit, and the eyes were now milky white. Destroyed.

Cicoi suspected he had lost two of his own eyestalks, but he did not care to think of that. Not yet. He made his crew pocket their damaged eyestalks and pull out only the stalks that they needed. Then he commanded that the interior light be raised slightly so that his crew could operate with fewer eyestalks extended.

The use of energy was probably extravagant, but he needed to keep his staff focused on the task ahead.

Whatever that may be.

He had to focus on it as well, but he could barely get past the explosion.

Such a waste of energy.

And such power.

He suspected that the blast they had used on the station was similar to the ones they had used on Malmur.

The destruction had been terrible. He'd lost one entire ship and two others had been damaged with debris. The commanders believed they could get the ships back to Malmur, but it would take all of their energy and all of their effort.

The third planet dominated his viewscreen like a malevolent blue-and-white ball. Once its very brightness had seemed like salvation. Now it seemed sinister to him.

Not only had the creatures struck the first blow in this new exchange, they had also created another problem.

There were more explosives heading toward Malmur. And he could not be complacent. He knew that they were the same as before—explosives that would not detonate until impact.

They had to be blown out of space before they reached Malmur. There were over a hundred of them. Fifteen had damaged the surface badly. A hundred would destroy the entire planet.

His upper tentacles tightened around his torso. He could feel the dry flakes peeling off. The stress of all of this was destroying him, too. But he could not afford to concentrate on himself. Not while Malmur was in danger.

The creatures were brilliant. He had never thought of that before, but they were. They were trying to force him to return to Malmur without taking a harvest.

But he could not.

He dared not.

He did not have enough food and energy for the long darkness. His people would die either way.

Why had no one known how intelligent the third planet's creatures were? Why had no one realized that they would develop into such powerful adversaries?

The Elder floated before him, a blackness against the viewscreen. Other members of the crew saw him and pocketed their eyestalks.

The Elder's shadowy shape approached Cicoi's command position.

So, the Elder spoke inside his head. *They have surprised you again.*

And you, Cicoi thought. *You did not expect this.*

I expected something.

Not here, not in space, Cicoi thought. *You did not expect this or you would have warned me.*

The Elder's upper tentacles floated with irritation. *You are angry with me.*

I am angry, Cicoi thought. *They have bested us again.*

Not entirely. The Elder seemed calmer than Cicoi

was. Cicoi hated that. The Elder should have been upset at all of the destruction. *They only best us if they take us off our course.*

We cannot let them attack Malmur.

That is Malmur's problem, the Elder said. *They will have to solve this from the ground.*

We left them nothing to solve it with. Cicoi's own upper tentacles floated. He had never been this angry, not with an Elder. *They have no ships, no leaders. They will not know until it is too late. Then what are we harvesting for?*

The Elder studied him for a moment. Cicoi felt the Elder's presence in his mind like a loud whisper. Moving and irritating at the same time.

You have experience fighting these creatures, Cicoi, the Elder said. *Use it.*

And then the Elder faded away as if he had never been. Cicoi could no longer feel him in his mind. But that didn't stop Cicoi from attempting to speak to him.

What do you mean? Cicoi asked. *What do you mean?*

But there was no response. For a long moment, Cicoi stared at the explosives, heading toward his home, and felt his tentacles wilt. His two eyestalks were throbbing now, and he was seeing light through them even though they were pocketed. He had suffered some sort of damage. He simply didn't have time to evaluate it.

"Contact home," he said to his Second. "Tell them of the explosives headed toward them. Tell them to choose a leader from the remaining males and have that leader contact the Keepers of the Stored Memories. See what planetary defenses Malmur once used. They will have to use them again."

"We have no systems for that," the Second said.

Cicoi flicked a tentacle in irritation. "Of course not. But if we do not develop one, we will not have a home."

The Second lowered himself as best he could. It was impossible to flatten the lower tentacles in this command center, but the Second did admirably well. Still, Cicoi did not forgive him for the question.

"Command Third," Cicoi said, "contact the Commanders of the North and Center. Tell them to send one ship each in pursuit of those explosives. We will send one as well. All three ships *must* be fighters, and they *must* destroy those explosives before they get to Malmur."

The Third lowered his eyestalks in acknowledgment.

The Second had risen, and he was moving his upper tentacles across his control board, preparing to contact home.

"Second," Cicoi said, "there are several ships still at home that we were unable to finish repairing before this trip. Tell the lead male to finish them. There should be enough time. Those ships must be launched at these explosives. Not one explosive must get through. Is that clear?"

"Yes," the Second said, lowering himself again.

Cicoi surveyed his crew. They all had one eyestalk

partially out, watching him. They had all lowered themselves slightly, feeling his displeasure.

Beyond them, the blue-and-white ball loomed.

"These creatures will have many more surprises for us," Cicoi said, "but we cannot allow them to defeat us. We shall prevail."

He spread his upper tentacles. "Tell the Commanders of the North and Center to split their ships into their harvesting position. Remind them to use the energy shields. We must take as much energy from them as we can, and we must not let them harm us. If the Commanders have questions, send them to me."

"I am honored to fulfill your request," the Second said.

Cicoi felt the tip of his upper tentacles wave in surprise. No one had used formal language with him since he started his command. Even though he held the position, he had not had the practical experience. Apparently his crew thought he did now.

It was a small comfort, but it was a comfort nonetheless. He would get them through this. He would protect his ships and his home.

November 10, 2018
4:38 A.M. Eastern Standard Time

Second Harvest: First Day

General Clarissa Maddox stood in the back of the war room, feet slightly apart. The exhaustion she had felt for the last few weeks had vanished. Nothing existed for her except those alien ships orbiting Earth.

She had destroyed one and injured others. She couldn't tell how badly, but she knew, she *knew,* the aliens hadn't expected Earth to take the offensive. She thought she sensed a hesitation in them. She knew they would be cautious in their approach.

Her team, most of them seated at desks, monitoring the information being sent from around the globe, had cheered when the ISS exploded, taking one alien vessel with it.

She hadn't. She knew that was one small victory in what was going to be a long, ugly war.

At least she was ready for it.

She was in the bunker beneath the White House, a bunker that extended for miles. She had brought the Tenth Planet Project into one small corner for its last meeting—a calculated gamble, one designed to show the U.S. members that the military was not going to play around with anyone's future. She had a hunch that Cross caught that, and no one else. Everyone else had seemed baffled by the fresh food and the high-tech equipment.

There was fresh food in this room as well. Maddox knew her staff wasn't going to get any sleep, not with those alien bastards circling up above, so she made sure there was enough food for everyone. She would have ordered sleeping shifts as well—and if this fight lasted longer than Cross's people predicted, she would—but right now, she wanted her best staff on alert and ready. A lot of caffeine would do it, caffeine and food whenever anyone got hungry.

So far, no one had gotten hungry, not since those damned aliens arrived.

To her left, muted vid commentators explained what was going on in Earth's orbit. Every major channel and some minor ones were on. Some of her staff were monitoring the net as well, even though she had mostly mandated the Tenth Planet Project to do that. She hoped against hope that the aliens had learned a human language and were going to download some information somewhere.

She knew that was an impossible dream, but that didn't stop her from having it.

Before her was an illuminated holographic map of the world. It accurately depicted how the Earth looked, all the way down to which parts were in darkness and which parts were in sunlight. It rotated much faster than Earth did, though. And her great programmers had somehow replicated the alien ships in orbit. As well as the satellites and other debris that Earth put up there.

Fortunately, for her and her staff, no one had depicted the shuttle. She had learned, not a half hour ago, that the *Endeavor II* was not responding to hails. All indications were that the aliens had sucked the energy out of the ship before their own craft had exploded.

She supposed Banks could dead-stick the shuttle in, but that meant a thousand things had to go right. And Maddox didn't have time to believe that the universe would line up that way, not even for someone as competent as General Gail Banks.

To Maddox's right were the available vid images from space. One of the screens was now fuzzy, a blur of nonreception. She hadn't ordered her staff to shut it off yet. That screen had once showed the view from the ISS. That camera had been destroyed. She knew her staff was seeing that as a victory, so she wasn't complaining about the waste of visuals.

She was trying to concentrate on the aliens' next move.

"We got it," said her chief of staff, Paul Ward. "They're separating out."

Maddox bent over her own screen, touching its cool surface so that she got the same readout he did. The alien fleet was splitting into three parts, just as it had before.

She felt her heart jump, then tried to calm herself. No sense getting excited, not yet. But she wanted to kiss Leo Cross. He had told her the aliens would be predictable, and they were proving it, first by how they entered orbit, and now by separating into three units, just like before.

She glanced up. The holographic simulation had caught it as well. The ships were splitting up, heading to different parts of the Earth. One unit stopped over a fertile area of Vietnam and Laos. Another stopped over the Amazon—again!—and a third over a heavily wooded area of British Columbia, Canada.

She felt the muscles in her shoulders tighten as she waited, waited to see if the ships moved on.

They did not.

She let out a small breath of air. No cities. The ships weren't stopping over the cities.

Cross had been right. The aliens needed food more than revenge.

Food and survival.

Predictable.

Maddox resisted the urge to pump her fist into the air. They hadn't won yet. They really hadn't even started.

She took a deep breath. She was in charge of this attack, thanks to her success against the aliens last spring.

She would make this work.

"All right," Maddox said to Ward. "Let's get this coordinated. We need to notify all the jets and small planes in the areas where the ships are coming down that they're going to have to implement Plan Alpha. Make sure we have enough ships patrolling those areas."

She said that last as a precaution. She had ordered more planes into the unpopulated areas, but she wasn't sure if some of the foreign countries had carried out that order. She hoped they had, because those planes had to be in the air already, patrolling.

They wouldn't do anything until after the aliens had dropped the harvesters and were coming back to pick them up. Then the planes would drop the adhesive bombs on top of the ships and get out of the area. When the ships climbed to the proper altitude, a lever inside the bomb would trigger and explode.

Simple, neat, and efficient.

All that Maddox could ask for.

"We're going to lose a lot of countryside," Ward said. "I still think we should drop one unit of nanorescuers to see if they really do defeat the harvesters."

"They've worked in test after test. And we're not going to tip our hands. Not when they're so close," Maddox said. Then she turned to him. "I gave you an order, mister."

He saluted smartly, his face coloring. He had clearly been caught up in the what-ifs, just like she had. He turned and headed toward the senior staff, relaying her orders.

She gazed at the holographic replicas of the ships, forming like black storm clouds over their selected regions.

"Think you can steal from us and get away with it, you bastards?" she muttered. "You wait. You just wait and see what we have in store for you."

7

November 10, 2018
9:41 Universal Time

Second Harvest: First Day

One problem at a time, General Gail Banks re-
minded herself as her fingers shook over the controls.
The controls were useless, but she wanted to keep
movement in her fingers. If they froze up on her, she
wouldn't be able to use them when she needed them.

Her skin was red and it ached. She wished she had
taken that extra few minutes to put on a space suit. She
was in her uniform, but it wouldn't provide enough
protection against the cold.

How long could a human survive in deep cold? If
she remembered her biology correctly, a person could
survive for quite a while—but not awake.

She would fall asleep long before the cold killed her.

The problem was that she didn't dare fall asleep.

She could see her breath and her copilot's, Sofia
Razi's, too. Behind them, Michael Thorne was breath-

ing loudly. Banks could hear the panic in every breath. She was glad she was at the helm of this shuttle. Something in Thorne's demeanor told her he wouldn't have made it this far.

One problem at a time.

She had to stop thinking about the cold. The cold would cease to be an issue the moment they entered the atmosphere. In fact, then they'd have to worry about burning to death. Nothing about space was easy. Everything was extremes. It was what she loved about it.

She wondered how the rest of her crew was doing in the back. They were used to the extremes of space, as well. Most of them had been trained in hands-on flying—every astronaut still had to have flight training—but most of them hadn't done it for a long time. And most of them hadn't worked in conditions that required creativity, at least not since training school.

Banks didn't want to think about how long it had been since she had had to improvise like this.

The *Endeavor II* shuddered as if it were hitting something hard. The frost on the windows instantly melted.

Banks felt her breath catch in her throat. They had just hit the very thin, upper edge of the atmosphere. And from the looks of the redness around them, they were going in.

Now it was time to face the next problem. Banks steadied herself. For the next few minutes she had to do the best flying of her life.

"Sure wish we had a way of knowing if the manual hydraulics were going to work," Razi said.

Banks agreed. They would have to let the design of the shuttle carry them down and slow their momentum before the hydraulics would even work. Right now, the shuttle was like a falling meteor, hitting the atmosphere at a high rate of speed. At least it seemed as if they were coming in flat, which was helping.

The bright red and orange air smashing past the shuttle heated everything. The tiles on the underside of the shuttle were protecting them from the heat of the friction of reentry. But it wasn't keeping the interior regulated in the normal way. The environmental controls were gone.

Banks felt sweat break out on her forehead, arms, and back. Pain shot through her numb fingers and toes, a sensation she hadn't felt since her childhood when she had stayed outside too long in the cold, wet snow, and then plunged her feet into a hot bathtub. She kept moving her fingers, knowing she'd need them.

Razi's face had grown red.

"We're not going to make it through this," Thorne said.

"Get in the back," Banks said.

"The odds—"

"I don't need to hear the odds or your pessimism. Get in the back."

Thorne shot her a glance and didn't move. "You'll need me."

"That's more optimistic," she said. "You can stay as long as you shut up."

He nodded his head. Razi stifled a grin. Banks pulled off her coat and stripped down to her T-shirt.

She longed to take off her shoes as well, but knew that wouldn't be practical. Even her hair was suddenly wet with sweat.

She wished she had a clock so she would know how much longer this would last. Minutes seemed like an eternity in here. This was one problem she had no control over. She had to trust her ship. It was built sturdy enough to get them through without cooking the crew like lobsters in boiling water.

She raised her fingers away from the controls. Even the plastic surfaces were growing too hot to touch. Any more heat and everything inside would start melting. Her throat was so dry it hurt. She should have brought water up here, but she would bet that the water stored in the back was too hot to touch.

Finally, the reds outside the window started fading.

"We're slowing down," Razi said.

Banks could feel it, too. Son of a bitch! She laughed and heard a hysterical edge to her voice. "We did it."

Thorne started cheering, and behind her, she heard other voices cheering as well.

"We did it," Banks repeated.

Razi was grinning.

But they didn't have much time to celebrate. They had made it through the friction of reentry. Now they had to land this thing.

The next problem.

Banks felt her giddiness ease. She looked at the control wheel in front of her. It had been installed in just this shuttle alone. She had specifically asked for *En-*

deavor II when she heard the plans for the ISS, because she knew the *Endeavor II* had more manual equipment than any other shuttle.

Now she was glad she had seen that far ahead.

The wheel was a lot like the old steering wheels on planes. It controlled the manual hydraulic system that had been installed in the shuttle. If she turned the wheel to the right, it increased the pressure in certain hydraulic lines and the rudder went left, moving the glider slightly to the right.

Pull back on the wheel, ship up slightly. But the shuttles were never intended to be controlled in this way. In the test flights even the *Endeavor II* had worked only marginally. Just good enough, one of the engineers had said, to give the best damn pilots a chance to survive.

Well, she was one of the best damn pilots. And she was taking every chance she could.

She was going to flare the nose up slightly right before the *Endeavor* plowed into the ground.

Finding a landing strip was going to be impossible, simply because they didn't have the computers to figure out how to plan the glide approach to it.

She put her hands on the wheel. It was still hot, like the interior of a car is after sitting in the sun on a blistering summer day. She had trouble bending her fingers, but she forced them, despite the pain.

A bead of sweat trickled down the side of her face.

"I need eyes," she said.

"I got it," Thorne said, but it was Razi who unbuckled and stood so that she could get a better sight line out of the front windows of the shuttle, past the nose. Thorne apparently didn't move at all.

Slowly Banks eased the nose down to a more level glide angle.

The shuttle responded to her control like an old cow trying to be shoved into a barn. Slowly . . . slowly . . .

One problem at a time.

Sweat stung her eyes, and she brushed at it with her right shoulder. Thorne saw the problem and wiped her brow with a tissue.

"Thanks," she said, marveling that such a small gesture could actually change her opinion of someone.

"We're over the Atlantic," Razi said. "The east coast of North America is straight ahead."

Damn it all to hell, Banks thought. The United States was the worst place she could land. There were too many people. And she didn't dare ditch in the ocean. The crew would never get out before the shuttle sank.

"Florida," Banks said. "We can head there."

"Or Texas," Razi said. "Lots of flat lands there."

"Not flat enough," Banks said, suddenly knowing what she wanted to try. "I'm going to make a long pass down Florida's Gulf Coast, then see if I can make a turn and bring the shuttle down on a straight beach."

The copilot nodded. "Good thinking. We miss and the water's warm and shallow."

Banks nodded. "And flat."

"It's like having a runway and a backup runway." Thorne sounded relieved.

He was premature. She still had half a hundred steps to go through before they got off this ship and walked on terra firma again.

She eased the shuttle into a banking turn south, the hydraulic rudders working smoothly for the moment. The shuttle might be heavy, but in the atmosphere, it was a decent glider. And extremely fast.

Banks could see that the sun hadn't yet got to the eastern seaboard, which would help them. They could see the outline of the land, and also lights along the shoreline.

The minutes ticked by as they sped half the length of Florida. Banks guessed that they were at thirty thousand feet when Razi said, "Better make the final turn."

Banks agreed, slowly easing the shuttle to the left. In front of her the dark Gulf of Mexico loomed. Then slowly the coast of western Florida came back into sight, and she straightened their path along the seemingly straight edge. She knew that beach and shoreline were far from straight, but it was the best they could do at this point. She could get it down, but from that point onward, it was going to be sheer luck that saved them.

Luck had been with them so far. She would help it along by keeping this beast as straight as she could.

"Coming up fast," Razi said.

"Get buckled in," Banks said, then shouted back to the rest of the crew, "Hold on tight! This is going to be rough!"

Ahead of her she could see the dark line that indicated small waves and black water lapping on the sands. Houses, roads, tiny towns were flashing by behind them as they came in at nearly 200 mph.

At what seemed like around a thousand feet, she pulled back on the wheel, pulling the nose up and aiming the shuttle just along the wave line. For a moment she thought she had acted too late as the ground and water rushed up at them. But then the nose of the shuttle came up slightly, blocking her view of what was ahead.

Holding the wheel as tight and as hard as she could, she waited, keeping the shuttle straight.

Her muscles strained and shook. The sweat pasted her T-shirt to her back. She had to remind herself not to hold her breath.

Time stretched.

The impact seemed to take forever.

Out the side window, lights flashed past faster than she wanted to imagine.

Then suddenly she was smashed forward against her safety harness.

Scrapes, and squeals, and shattering, thundering crashes echoed around her.

The screaming of metal against sand made goose bumps rise on her flesh.

She clung to the wheel with all of her strength, focusing on holding the shuttle straight. It had to stay straight, but it was like controlling a herd of elephants with her bare hands.

Then for an instant the shuttle seemed to stop.

And in that instant, she knew what had happened. The shuttle had skipped like a flat stone over water.

Skipped as it had been designed to do in the upper atmosphere.

But this wasn't the upper atmosphere. This was hard water and beach they had just skipped back into the air on.

"Shit!" she shouted.

She fought to hold the wheel in a position she thought was straight.

Fought to keep the nose straight down the beach.

Then she saw the lights of beach homes flash past her window. She had lost. The shuttle wasn't straight at all. She fought the wheel, fought and fought—

As it turned out, there was nothing she could have done.

The shuttle's wing caught the sand, twisting the shuttle around and flipping it like a spinning top down the dark beach.

The spinning tore the shuttle apart, scattering tiles and parts as it tumbled down the beach at over two hundred miles per hour.

Everyone inside was killed instantly, the force of the impact ripping them apart and splattering them around the cabin.

Two miles later the last small intact section of the shuttle cabin finally exploded on impact into a concrete beach wall.

There were only a few witnesses to the final moments of the shuttle as almost everyone who lived along that stretch of Gulf beach had evacuated the area for Orlando.

November 10, 2018
6:55 A.M. Central Standard Time

Second Harvest: First Day

Kara Willis's back hurt. She was sitting on the ruined stool again, but the curve of the leather seat pushed the stool away from the wall just enough so that she couldn't lean back comfortably. She had been on the stool most of the night.

The Hendricksons had fallen asleep on the couch, and her mother hadn't let her wake them. Mr. Nelson sat in her father's La-Z-Boy, and Barb was rocking in her mother's rocker. Her mother was still in the kitchen, working frantically. She had refused to come into the living room to see what was happening. Instead, she was cooking as if there would be no tomorrow.

The phrase made Kara shudder. That was what they had been facing all along. No tomorrow. That was why she and half the household had stayed up all night.

Her father had wandered in and out of the room as the night progressed, stopping long enough to stare at the television, and then shaking his head and walking away. He didn't like to be out of control any more than her mother did. And he hated what this had reduced them to—not the family so much as humanity itself.

He felt that human beings had stopped living while this threat was going on. They were just surviving, he had said, and that made them little more than animals. Kara had asked about the people leading the countries,

170

the people who were fighting the aliens, and he had said they were surviving, too, just on a different level.

His attitude was so dark, so negative, that she didn't really want to be near him. And fortunately it was fairly easy to stay away while there were so many people in the house.

She had been watching the various channels for several hours now. When the harvesters finally fell over places she had never cared about, Vietnam and Laos, and one place she had only visited, British Columbia, she felt a mixture of relief and terror. Relief that nothing was landing on Chicago, and terror that something would.

There were no nanorescuers in those wild places, so she wasn't going to find out if the "protection" worked. Not yet anyway. And the newscasters were promising that the humans would attack the aliens when they came back to pick up their harvesters. That wasn't going to be for twelve hours or more—full dark.

The sun was just beginning to rise here. Kara could see pinkness on the horizon through the living room picture window. She pushed herself off the stool and went to the door.

"Where're you going, honey?" her mother asked.

Kara didn't answer. She stepped outside, leaving the door open, and stared at the east.

The sunrise was pink and orange, with some dark red mixed in. What was that old saying? *Red in the morning, sailors take warning.* There was red here.

She took a deep breath. A lot of her neighbors were still outside, some of them asleep in their lawn chairs,

171

blankets covering them. Most of the tents were zipped closed, and she couldn't see the occupants.

She was the only one watching the sunrise. Even though it might be the last sunrise they ever see.

Her mother had told her not to be so pessimistic. Pessimism, her mother said, never got them anywhere. Yet it had been her mother who had sobbed so badly when she heard the aliens were returning, her mother who couldn't watch the vids now, her mother who was trying to cook enough food to feed an army, maybe with the thought that, after today, they might never get a chance to eat again.

Kara shuddered. It was cold and damp. A November morning. That threat of snow she had felt the night before was still in the air, but there were no clouds, at least not yet. Something about the chill told her that winter was here. She usually hated winter.

She wanted to see this one.

Those people on the shuttle wouldn't. Mr. Nelson had turned up the sound on one of the screens when the vid reporter was talking about the shuttle crew. They'd gotten off the International Space Station, blown it up and taken some aliens with it, survived the reentry into the atmosphere, and missed the landing on the beach. Up until that moment, the commentators were calling the crew's survival a miracle and a sign.

After that, they had shut up.

But Kara was wondering if it was a sign. A sign that everything would go really well until the last minute, and then no one on Earth would know what hit them.

After all, the aliens didn't need humans. They needed trees and plants and stuff, from what she'd been hearing. They needed to take stuff from the Earth so that they could live. Like farmers, only the aliens didn't grow anything. The ultimate hunter-gatherers, her father had called them.

If Kara was those aliens, and she knew that humans could kick her butt, she'd do everything she could to destroy humans and leave Earth intact.

She hoped the governments and the military had thought of that and were guarding against it. Because there was a part of Kara that believed all this talk about one more harvest after this one, only one more, was wrong.

She didn't know where the feeling came from. Her father would say it came from her fear.

Maybe he was right. After all, the Earth was a pretty big place. Even if the aliens came back again and again, they might not try to destroy Chicago. She had a really good chance of surviving.

"Kara, you're letting in the cold!" Her mother's voice floated from inside.

Kara sighed and looked at the sunrise one last time. It was beautiful. Would it still be that beautiful if there were no people left to enjoy it?

It was a question she'd never know the answer to, no matter what happened.

All she knew was that she wanted to see another sunrise. Thousands of sunrises. All the sunrises that she, as a seventeen-year-old girl, was entitled to.

Those aliens didn't have the right to take that away.

November 10, 2018
11:10 P.M. Eastern Standard Time

Second Harvest: First Day

All day and all night. Cross had managed to catch a two-hour nap on his couch midmorning, after Britt threatened to conk him with a chair and put him out herself. He'd agreed to take the nap as long as she took one, too, and they'd both agreed not to take one at the same time because he would have wagered neither of them would have slept.

Not that holding Britt for two hours would have been bad, but they needed the rest. They had to be on their toes for the next part of this whole attack.

Now Cross was sitting on the corner of the desk where, almost twenty-four hours earlier, he had watched as the shuttle left the ISS. The loss of Banks and her crew had shaken him more than he wanted to admit. He blamed his reaction on lack of sleep, but he actually thought that he had felt so strongly because they had been so heroic, and they had come so close.

It hadn't been fair, but nothing about the tenth planet had been fair. He thought it monstrously unfair that he understood why the aliens were coming here. If only they were truly evil, inexplicable things who had attacked the Earth for no reason. But Cross understood their need to harvest the Earth's riches. If he were in their situation, he would have tried to find a solution, any solution, no matter what the cost.

Just as they had.

And until now, they had probably thought the humans one more primitive race on a primitive world. A lot had changed in two thousand years.

"My God," someone said.

Cross blinked. He'd almost been asleep on the corner of the desk, lost in his reverie. Before him, the telemetry continued to pour onto the screens, and the visuals didn't look a lot different.

Everyone in the room, though, was looking at Odette Roosevelt. She had her hand over her mouth. Britt was hurrying to her side.

"What is it?" Britt asked.

"They're coming back for their harvesters," Roosevelt said.

Cross stood. Everyone else around him was standing, too, trying to see, on the small television monitors, the battle that they'd all be waiting for.

But Cross shoved his way forward. "Are you sure?" he asked.

Roosevelt nodded.

"They're early," he said to Britt. She frowned at him, not understanding why he was so concerned.

He kissed her on the cheek and headed back to his own office, muttering to himself the whole way. During the first harvest, the aliens had left the harvesters on the ground for more than twenty-three hours. This time they had cut that time short by five hours.

Why?

He pulled open his office door, stepped over the pile of cups and paper plates that were spilling out of his garbage can, and climbed behind his desk.

This wasn't right. The aliens were supposed to be predictable. And this wasn't.

Something was wrong.

He had to find out what that was as fast as he could.

He had a hunch there was not a lot of time left.

THE FINAL
SHOT

8

November 10, 2018
8:14 P.M. Pacific Standard Time

Second Harvest: First Day

Finn Broderick held the controls of the Gulfstream 4 and marveled at the fact that he was doing this. Once upon a time, he'd been a commuter pilot, bringing people in and out of the Alaskan wilderness. A glam job, he'd thought when he lived in Florida. A nasty tough job, he'd learned when he got here, and one he'd been doing for nearly fifteen years. Doing, and doing well.

He just never expected to do it in a war.

His copilot, Wyatt Crowfield, was a native Alaskan who thought this whole thing was an adventure. He was a lean man who didn't speak much. He let his scars speak for him. His entire face had been lacerated by a momma grizzly when he'd been twelve. He had barely survived. The fact that he had survived made him something of a legend in these parts—and somehow got him a lot of women.

Finn had no idea what the women saw in that mutilated face, but they saw something. Wyatt never wanted for a midnight companion.

And he certainly wouldn't if tonight's work went as planned.

Finn was circling at just under ten thousand feet. His jet was empty—no passengers sitting in those plush, expensive seats. The only customer on this flight was one bomb strapped below his cockpit, and it wasn't even a paying customer. Although he never hoped a job would go as well as this one.

They'd been circling for an hour now inland from Juneau. The bowl where Juneau sat looked like home to him. On the other side of the coastal mountain range where he was circling, British Columbia loomed. But not the British Columbia he had known for the last fifteen years. A place that was now as unfamiliar as the moon.

The aliens' harvesters had turned that lush forest land into a sea of black dust. Until the light faded, he could see the dust from his cockpit. Now he thought he imagined it, a thin line in the darkness, a line that was even blacker than anything around him.

The aliens weren't expected to return yet, but dozens and dozens of planes were in the air nearby, all different, all equipped with a bomb—a very powerful focused charge—ready to drop on the alien ships. Even more planes would take to the air when the expected time arrived. He hoped by then to have returned to Juneau, refueled, and gotten back in the air.

"She-it," Wyatt said, the word half a whistle.

"What?" Finn asked. He didn't like the idea of anything going differently than planned.

"They're coming down."

"The alien ships?"

"No, the stars."

Finn let out a nervous breath. "They weren't due back for hours."

"You want to beam them that message?" Wyatt asked. "Or should we just hope they got the memo?"

Finn took a deep breath. Wyatt was clearly as nervous as he was. Wyatt only got sarcastic when he was nervous or drunk. And Finn knew Wyatt wasn't drunk.

"What's the alien bastard closest to our position?" Finn asked.

"Forty miles, hovering at just under five thousand feet."

He turned the plane toward the coordinates that Wyatt gave him.

They zoomed toward it, Finn's breath coming in short gasps. He'd felt this way the first time he'd seen Alaska's backcountry, how large and empty it was, and how beautiful.

Only now he wasn't heading toward beauty. He was heading to destroy something. Something that would have destroyed him first if he let it.

"Je-zus, Finn," Wyatt said, another whistle in his

voice. "TCAS shows there must be a hundred different planes heading toward those alien ships."

"Where's air traffic control when you need them?" Finn muttered. He'd never been in such crowded airspace. "How many are going to get there before us?"

"Maybe one or two." Wyatt grinned, his face green in the light from the cockpit instruments. He looked like the Grinch on speed.

"Let's hope the rest of them are paying attention," Finn said.

It seemed to take forever to reach the alien ship's coordinates, but in truth it only took a matter of minutes.

"You use TCAS and radar and eyeball stuff as well," Finn said. "I'm not getting close to any of our own guys."

"Don't worry," Wyatt said. "I live a charmed life."

"I hope to God that's true," Finn said. He'd always been afraid that surviving the bear had used all of Wyatt's luck.

They were right on top of the coordinates, but Finn couldn't see the huge ship below him in the dark. He knew it was there, though. He could feel it, like a ghastly poisonous shape stalking him in the night. His hands were slick on the controls. He'd never been this close to evil before.

His instructions were to stay at least two thousand feet above the ship. They were supposed to time their drop with radar, using their slowest stable airspeed.

And then just hope.

As the person who briefed them had said, even if

one out of ten bombs hit and stick, that would be enough to hurt an alien ship.

Well, he had only one bomb, and he was going to make it work. He only got one shot at these ugly mothers, and he was going to give it all he could.

"Coming up on the target," Wyatt said.

Finn relaxed. They were in routine now. "Count me down."

"Thirty seconds," Wyatt said.

They had practiced this routine a dozen times, both with daylight and night drops, hitting a huge circle the size of an enemy ship with dummy bombs. At night they had hit the target from two thousand feet three out of seven tries. Tonight would be number four.

He desperately wanted to take them in closer, but he'd been sternly lectured that going any closer would destroy the plane and get them killed. And that would do Earth's cause no good at all. The aliens were going to make another raid. Earth needed the plane in one piece and ready to bomb again.

Still he was tempted to dive in lower, make sure he delivered the bomb on target. He wouldn't have gotten where he was without taking risks.

"Ten seconds," Wyatt said.

Too late to do it this time. Next time.

"Five."

Finn's heart was pounding.

"Four."

His finger found the release.

"Three."

These seconds seemed to take forever.

"Two."

He braced himself. This was what he had trained for.

"One."

He glanced at Wyatt, who was concentrating.

"Go!"

Finn pressed. He could feel the bomb release from the plane. He waited a moment, then turned, banking away and back toward base to get quickly out of the way of the other planes coming in to make similar attack runs.

It was a sea of running lights and wings and blips on the radar screen. He flew as best he could, given the traffic.

"Well?" he asked, as Wyatt tracked the bomb.

The seconds dragged past.

"Well?"

"Got it!" shouted Wyatt. "Direct hit. We got it!"

Finn let out air he hadn't even known he had been holding. He fought to remain calm, knowing he had some flying left to do. "Let's just hope the damn thing stuck. I want to see the explosion when those bastards reach forty thousand feet."

He took the jet back toward Juneau and resumed his tight circle pattern. He'd stay up out here as long as fuel allowed, just hoping for the sight of that thing exploding.

He wasn't disappointed.

Eighteen minutes later, the night sky lit up with a flare that was as bright as dawn.

One alien ship gone.

And in all his life he had never felt so proud.

Second Harvest: Second Day

Cicoi's two damaged eyestalks were permanently stuck in their pockets. They felt swollen and they ached, a constant distraction from the task before him.

His lower tentacles were wrapped around the command circle, his uppers spread on the controls. His remaining eyestalks were extended, watching the surface of the third planet, as if he could see all the details.

Of course he couldn't.

But he knew them.

Twenty-six ships had been destroyed, all harvest ships. So many others had been damaged.

The creatures were more inventive than even he had thought. Who would have imagined that they found a delivery system for explosives that didn't get snared in the energy shield?

Their attack had been brilliant and beautifully executed, and he had given them the time. The very system—the Sulas on the ground, harvesting as they had done each Pass before—had shown the creatures where to bring their weapons. They had attacked at the right moment, and somehow their weapons had worked even though they were not close by.

It had been brilliant and devastating. Thousands of his people would die of starvation because of this single disaster.

And he was running out of time.

At home, at least, plans were going well. He had received word that six ships would be ready to launch at the explosive devices the creatures had sent toward Malmur. The three ships he had sent after the devices would catch them before they were able to attack the planet's surface.

The Elder appeared before him like an angry wraith. Cicoi did not know how long the Elder had been there, listening to his thoughts.

The Elder slipped beside Cicoi in the command position. Cicoi did not move out of the way as he once would have.

We must strike back, the Elder said.

We already have a plan, Cicoi thought. He no longer felt qualms about challenging the Elder.

The Elder didn't even seem to hear him. *We can gain more energy and materials from attacking their population centers. We must not allow them to do this to us again.*

Cicoi felt shock roll through him. Had the Elder lost his sense of their mission? *These creatures have come a long way since our last Pass. They are not the same creatures that we saw after our last sleep. They have gone from being primitives to gaining space travel. Do you actually think they will still be devastated by our attack the next time our planet comes close to them?*

The Elder floated away from the command center. *We will make them remember. We will hurt them so badly they will never recover.*

To do that, Cicoi said, *we must devastate their world. It is our best source of food.*

You do not understand war, the Elder said.

"No," Cicoi actually spoke aloud, something he hadn't done with the Elder in months. "You do not understand us any longer. We are not people who live in a straight time line any more. We live interrupted lives. You have forgotten that."

And you have forgotten respect.

"Perhaps," Cicoi said. "But I know that fighting your way will destroy all of us."

His staff pocketed eyestalks and wrapped their tentacles around consoles in an attempt to ignore Cicoi's side of the conversation.

"We must get enough food to sustain as many of our people as we can," Cicoi said. "We will stay with the planned second targets."

The Elder hovered close. Cicoi had to fight to keep his upper tentacles still. He didn't want the Elder to see how nervous he was.

Cicoi had never stood up for himself before, but he had to now. The Elder's tactics were wrong, and if Cicoi followed them, he would doom his people forever.

We must not lose any more ships, the Elder said, but the words sounded petulant, as if he were upset at Cicoi for having the better idea.

We will not, Cicoi promised. *I have a plan. Once you showed me the weapons systems in the warships. Will they still work?*

Of course, the Elder said with pride. *They are tied to the propulsion systems. If propulsion works, weapons work.*

187

Cicoi pocketed three of his eyestalks. It was a nervous gesture and he wished he hadn't done it. The Elder might have seen the movement as weakness.

But, the Elder said, clearly noting Cicoi's gesture, *they use a lot of energy.*

Cicoi let his upper tentacles fall against his side. His staff's remaining eyestalks pocketed. Cicoi had made a command movement in front of an Elder, and the others wanted no part of it.

Better to use too much energy, Cicoi said, *than to lose more ships.*

The Elder floated before him, seemingly curious. *What do you propose?*

We must station the warships above the harvest ships, and when any of the creatures' ships fly near, we destroy them.

We do not absorb their energy? the Elder asked.

Cicoi felt as if he were being baited. *No. We use weapons. They will not expect it.*

This will be your decision. Its success or failure will rest on you.

Cicoi did not respond. There was nothing he could say. What the Elder failed to understand was that the decisions all had rested on Cicoi. The Elder's position was one as honored ancient, adviser and near-god. Cicoi was a young leader who was not being allowed to pay for his mistakes.

So all he could do was make certain there would be no others.

This seemed like the most logical choice.

When he did not respond to the Elder, the Elder

floated away and Cicoi could no longer see him. Still, Cicoi waited several moments before unpocketing his three eyestalks.

His Second saw Cicoi's movement, and unpocketed his remaining eyestalks. Slowly the other staff did the same. They seemed surprised that Cicoi was still before them, surprised that the Elder had not done something in retribution for Cicoi's lack of respect.

They had not heard the conversation. Most of it had occurred in Cicoi's mind. Most of the other conversations had occurred there, too. And what Cicoi was learning was that the Elder, while he had more experience, wasn't always right. The Elder still thought as if there was all the time in the universe, as if the Malmuria were millions strong, living on a planet that revolved around its own sun, and did not have to worry that a single error would cost thousands of lives.

Cicoi had to worry about such things. If he made too many mistakes, he would guarantee that his people would not survive the next darkness.

He would destroy his own race.

"Commander," his Second said, eyestalks turned away from him, "forgive the intrusion. But I have just received word that the Sulas are ready for another harvest."

It was time then. He used the tip of his fifth upper tentacle to summon the globe that represented the third planet. It appeared before him, rotating slowly, depicting the richest areas of the continents and the areas most populated by the third planet's sentient creatures.

Cicoi studied the surface, even though he had

picked out the targets before his ship had started orbiting the third planet.

"We will follow the plan as established earlier," Cicoi said to his Second. "Inform the Commanders of the North and Center."

His Second lowered his tentacles and flattened his eyestalks. Then he bent over his console to do Cicoi's bidding.

This was the most important harvest. Cicoi was determined to get through it without losing a single ship.

The third planet's creatures had surprised him for the final time.

November 11, 2018
5:19 P.M. Eastern Standard Time

Second Harvest: Second Day

Clarissa Maddox had allowed herself one undignified squeal of excitement when the first alien ship exploded. Her chief of staff, Paul Ward, had looked at her as if she had suddenly shouted obscenities in Mandarin Chinese. She was usually much more restrained than that.

But he seemed to be the only one who noticed her slip. The professional soldiers in the rest of the war room were jumping out of their seats, high-fiving each other, and screaming with excitement. She had done nothing to quell their enthusiasm. Her people needed a bit of joy after all that had happened.

The death of Gail Banks a few hours earlier had

made the room one of the most somber places Maddox had ever been in her life. She was pleased to see her people celebrating again.

The problem was it had taken nearly fifteen minutes to settle them down again, and fifteen minutes was too long. Yes, they had won a significant victory over the enemy ships. The battle was won, but she knew that winning battles did not always mean winning wars.

The aliens still had seventy-eight ships, and they were coming back for a second run.

This time, she didn't have surprise on her side.

She knew that would cost her something. She just wasn't sure what.

She stared at the holographic Earth in the center of the room and watched the dark alien ships, which had remained separated into three groups, in their new positions. They had devastated the areas they had covered before. She had no doubt they would do the same thing again.

This time, the ships were harvesting different areas than the first attack. The first group was in the Amazon, finishing off the last remaining section of the rainforest. Maddox hated watching this. Who knew how many species would disappear, how many important plants would die, how many people too primitive to know what was happening would disappear as well.

If only she had had more time to prepare.

If only.

The next group of ships was attacking Central Africa, several hundred miles south of the Sahara, into the Congo and the richest parts of the continent.

More species lost.

More lives lost.

And the third and final group of ships hovered over northern Minnesota and Canada, covering an area from the Superior National Forest into Ontario. They seemed to be avoiding Lake Superior and concentrating on the land.

Rich, rich farmland.

Maddox was just waiting for the right moment, when the alien crafts got low enough to pick up their deadly harvesters, low enough to be attacked.

On the screens to her left, commentators were babbling. Scenes of destruction flashed on the screens, followed by repeated footage of alien ships exploding.

Last night's victories.

Maddox wanted some more today.

"General, the first alien ships are moving into position."

Maddox nodded, studied the information coming across her own screens. All over the world, planes were waiting for her order.

Finally she gave it.

On the screens to her right, she got visuals from several of the planes in Minnesota. Her staff were giving her verbal updates. Hundreds upon hundreds of planes were in the air.

Then one of the lieutenants said, "What the hell?"

Maddox frowned. On the screens she saw only a black shape. She pressed the visual on the desk before her, froze the shape and reduced it in size until she was sure.

It was an alien craft, sleeker and darker than any of the others.

"What the hell is this thing?" she snapped.

"I don't know, sir," someone said.

"Then find out!"

And as she spoke, the dark ship opened fire on the planes, disintegrating them instantly.

Maddox glanced from screen to screen. The alien ships seemed to be protecting their harvesting ships at all three locations. Plane after plane was being shot from the sky.

"Maybe we should return fire?" one of the adjuncts asked.

"With what?" she snapped. "These are corporate jets and private planes and—ah, hell!"

And they were all dying before they could release their bombs.

"Call a retreat!" she said.

Her staff turned to her. She had vowed not to retreat before these aliens again. Her staff knew it. But she saw no choice. Most of those pilots were civilians and they were being slaughtered.

"Call the goddamn retreat!" she snapped.

And the word went out.

The planes retreated.

And the aliens were probably gloating.

"That son-of-a-bitch Cross said they'd conserve energy. That didn't seem like conservation to me." She was muttering as she touched the screen before her, getting updates.

"Actually, sir," Ward said, "it is. If you consider the ships to be a resource as well."

She shot him a look that she hoped would silence him for the rest of his life, then she sank into her chair.

The alien harvester ships were lowering to the proper altitude and retrieving their cloud of black dust.

She thought of how her family always went to the Superior National Forest in summer, and then drove around the lake to Michigan's Upper Peninsula. The nanoharvesters had fallen to Earth and ruined the place where she had once played as a child.

She clenched a fist and pounded it on the screen, causing all the images to jump or freeze.

This time the damned aliens had the benefit of surprise. She hadn't expected them to recover so quickly.

She had underestimated them.

And she couldn't get close to them, not with those weapons ships still hovering.

She had to think of something else.

At least this was the last attack.

At least they hadn't touched the cities.

There were small miracles here.

But not the miracles she wanted.

9

Second Harvest: Second Day

Kara got off the stool and walked toward the television screens. All the vid announcers were saying the same thing. The last attack had started, and the aliens had picked their targets.

The Amazon.

Africa.

And a state-and-a-half away from her. Close, but not close enough. She had known they were coming to the Midwest. She just hadn't expected it to be the upper Midwest and Canada.

She hoped that the folks in International Falls and Thunder Bay had evacuated like they were supposed to. She hoped they all got away safely.

She rested her hands on the back of the couch, not caring about the look she got from the Hendricksons.

So she was invading their personal space. *They* were invading her home.

Her mother had finally come out of the kitchen, a towel in her hands. She had flour on her cheek and a streak of chocolate near her upper lip. Her eyes were red-rimmed, just like they had been in the middle of the night when Kara had left her to return to the stool.

Some vid reporters were near the site. They were filming from the ground. A few were in helicopters, and Kara could hear tinny voices in the background, telling them they were in protected airspace.

"Idiots," her father said from behind her. "We don't need this on tape. We need to destroy those ships. That's the first priority."

"I think they have to be up there anyway," Mrs. Nelson said. "So they may as well film."

"At least we know what's going on." Barb was standing near the kitchen door. Kara had thought she had gone to bed long ago.

And Connor Hendrickson staggered out of his room, his long hair sticking up. He had actually been asleep. She glared at him. Yeah, he was good-looking, but what kind of guy slept when the world was about to be destroyed.

"We're okay then?" he asked.

"They missed us, son," his father said.

"Cool." Connor stuck his hands in the pocket of his robe and frowned at the screens. "Then what's that?"

An explosion occurred off to one side. Then another and another. There was screaming into the mikes. Mr. Nelson turned the sound up so loud Kara could hardly stand it.

"Shit!" her father said. "Those are our planes!"

"What's happening?" Barb asked, coming deeper into the room.

"People are dying," Kara's mother said, twisting the towel in her hands. "Oh, God."

She wandered back into the kitchen as if she couldn't stand what she was seeing. Kara couldn't either. Plane after plane was disappearing until, finally, the vids were cutting off.

Strained announcers were appearing on the screen again, and Kara leaned against the couch.

She had never felt so many conflicting emotions in her life. She was happy her home had been spared and relieved that she was going to live, and horrified, just horrified, that she had watched more people die.

Unlike her mother, she couldn't pull herself away from the screen. Those people had died defending the rest of the world. She had to know what took them out.

She was terrified that it was the aliens, that they had a new plan.

But she didn't say anything.

No sense in making everyone in the room feel worse.

November 12, 2018
7:46 A.M. Eastern Standard Time

Second Harvest: Third Day

Leo Cross pushed his chair away from his desk and watched the video monitor before him. The word "holding . . ." kept scrolling on the phone link. He knew he was holding, and he wasn't happy about it.

Maddox had promised him that he would be able to get through when he had a hunch—and this one was a doozy. He'd just gotten off the line with three different physicists. And they all confirmed what he had suspected.

This time, the aliens had a total of eighty-six hours before their best launch window forced them to return to the tenth planet. That was five hours longer than they had in April.

Cross thought about hanging up and dialing again. He'd done that twice, the last time shouting at the military officer who had answered the phone. The man who had informed him that "General Maddox was in the middle of something right now."

"I know that, goddammit," Cross had said. "Tell her Leo Cross has a hunch."

"Sir, I can't—"

"Tell her. I'm with the Tenth Planet Project. She knows who I am."

"Sir, I—"

"I'm the person who discovered the planet in the first place," Cross had snapped. "Now get her."

"Yes, sir," he'd said, and put Cross on hold. Cross hadn't called anyone from a large-screen video phone in years. He had forgotten how much more annoying it was to be put on hold when the word kept scrolling in front of him. When it scrolled on his wrist'puter, he didn't even notice.

This wasn't going to work. Dammit. He didn't have

time to drive across town, and he wasn't sure he would be able to find her. And damn Maddox for not giving him her personal line. She could have put him on hold as easily as that insufferable ass—

Then Cross sat up. The word "holding . . ." had disappeared, replaced with "transferring . . ." The ubiquitous ellipsis were almost as annoying as the scrolled words.

But the fact that he was being transferred had gotten his attention.

"Leo?" Maddox's face filled the screen. She looked flattened, distorted, and tired. He knew from the image that she was looking at her own 'puter.

"I think we need a secure line," he said.

"This is secure," she said.

"You might want to be alone."

She sighed and vanished from his view. He got a wrist's eye view of the room, upside down desks and screens and scurrying people.

Then they were in a hallway.

"Make it quick," she said. "I'm in the middle of a crisis."

"I know," he said. "My news is going to make it worse instead of better."

She didn't look surprised. "You said you had a hunch."

"I want to give you the thought process, so that you can see where I got this information."

She almost said no. He could see it in her face. Then she must have remembered how his other hunches worked, how unbelievable they had sounded without the explanation of how he had gotten there.

199

"This better be important," she said.

"Trust me, General," he said. "I wouldn't have bothered you if it wasn't."

She nodded.

He took a deep breath and plunged in. "All right. Here's how it goes. I told you the aliens were predictable."

"And you were wrong." She snarled the sentence. She blamed him, then, for the deaths.

"I still think they are. I think they're telling us—not intentionally—their plans through the changes they're making."

"You've got my attention," Maddox said.

"Last April," Cross said, "the aliens hit three different areas on their first attack. They left the harvesters on the planet's surface for almost twenty-four hours, then picked them up and retreated into orbit for another twenty-four hours. When they came back to harvest three more areas, it was just over twenty-four hours later. All in all, over four days, the aliens had been in orbit and harvesting just slightly over eighty hours. In that first attack, they had taken exactly half of what they had on their previous visits to Earth every 2006 years. That's how we knew they were coming back. That and the way their planet's orbit worked."

"I don't think I like where this is going," Maddox said.

Cross nodded. He didn't like it either, but that didn't change what he suspected was going to happen. He continued to explain his process. "You noted the changes," he said. "So did I. But there was something else that was different. This time, the aliens have eighty-six hours to harvest before they have to return to the tenth planet."

"Five hours longer than last time," she said softly.

"Yes," he said. "This time, their first attack took only eighteen hours. They waited eighteen hours between the first and second attacks."

Maddox looked at him, a frown line between her brows.

"If they pick up their nanoharvesters eighteen hours from when they started this second attack, they would have saved almost eighteen hours."

"Plus those extra five hours," Maddox said. "God-damn it. They're coming back for a third round, aren't they?"

"Yeah," Cross said.

"And these first two times we were lucky. They didn't go after the cities."

"That's right," Cross said.

"You think they'll do it this time?"

He shrugged. He'd been asking himself that very question and not getting any real answers. "We've hurt them time and time again. They don't have as many ships as they did. Maybe they need the third round just to get enough food to survive."

"Or?"

"They're using weapons on us, General," Cross said. "We're not the only ones who believe we're at war."

"I hate your hunches," she said. "But I'm damned glad you get them."

And then her image winked off.

Cross leaned back in the chair and caught his breath. He had relayed the information. He had done what he could.

But somehow, it didn't feel like he had done enough.

November 12, 2018
1:24 P.M. Eastern Standard Time

Second Harvest: Third Day

Clarissa Maddox had spent the last five hours preparing her planes, her people, and the diplomats for a possible third attack. For the first time in her career, she was happy to have diplomats around her. They got to tell the foreign governments the news she'd been repeating since she got off the phone with Leo Cross.

No one had taken it well.

Not even she had, if truth be told. Those damn aliens were making her extremely angry, and she had to figure out a way to make them pay for what they were doing.

She hadn't figured it all out yet. But she would. Cross wasn't the only person who had hunches.

She paced her small office beside the war room. She couldn't look at the holographic map of Earth at the moment, not with its gray spaces—from the aliens' April attack—and the black spaces that marked the damage they had done this time. The world looked like a patchwork quilt that someone had stained. And she took each damaged area very personally.

The problem was that Cross had been right. The aliens had left, taking their little nanoharvesters with them, and they had left after eighteen hours, just as he predicted. Which meant that the rest of his scenario was probably right, as well.

She didn't like it, but she would have to fight it, somehow. She just wasn't sure how.

No one knew how to get close to those death-ray spaceships the aliens had. And who knew they had those? Not even Leo Cross. He had been as surprised as she had.

Not that she could have done anything about them even if she had known.

Except save hundreds of human lives.

She had just under seventeen hours until those alien bastards came back, seventeen hours to come up with a plan before they damaged even more of the Earth's surface.

Seventeen hours.

Seemed like she had no time at all.

She couldn't even figure out where they were going to attack. Cross couldn't figure it either. Her own people couldn't tell if the aliens had enough food and supplies now or if this next run was to make up for all the damage that had been done.

She hoped that was what was going to happen, but she wasn't counting on anything.

Except the nanorescuers. She prayed to every god she could think of and some she probably couldn't that Portia Groopman's little invention worked as well *outside* the lab as it did inside. Because chances were at least one population center would get hit this time.

And then Maddox froze. The nanorescuers. They hooked into the alien harvesters. Maybe, just maybe, there would be a way to use that against the aliens.

She hit the space on her screen that got her a direct link with Leo Cross.

10

November 12, 2018
2:54 P.M. Central Standard Time

Second Harvest: Third Day

The house still didn't feel like her home. The furniture was rearranged, and there were gaping holes where other people's furniture had been. The hardwood floors were filthy, and the remotes were stained with soda and grease.

Kara's room still smelled like cheap perfume, even though her cousins were gone. And the back bedroom—the one that her mother was going to make into an office one day—reeked of dog pee. Apparently no one had let the puppies out for the last two days because they were afraid the dogs would die in the aliens' attack.

But the aliens had come and gone, and it was over. It was really and truly over.

All that was left, as her mother had said, was the cleanup.

And the repairs. Kara was supposed to be going through the house to see what was missing, what needed rearranging, and what needed their immediate attention. The dog pee certainly did, although she had no idea how to fix that. The basement was a mess, too. It had been trashed by the Nelsons, who apparently weren't as nice as they had seemed.

Only Barb was left. Barb and the Hendricksons, who didn't want to start the drive back home until the following day. Kara wished they would leave. She really couldn't face Connor again. Even if her mother said he—as a teenage boy—would be able to eat all the food she had cooked.

The kitchen looked like the holiday season was already upon them. Her mother had sent off their friends, relatives, and live-ins with a lot of baked goods and loaves of bread. So that they had something to eat when they got home, she had said, as if she had planned all of this.

Maybe she had, but Kara had never known her mother to be that optimistic.

She went into the new wing of the house, the one her father had added when he got promoted to senior partner at his law firm. Her grandparents had stayed here. Her parents called this wing the guest apartment, and it was sort of that, with its own little sitting room, the nice bedroom, and the really big bathroom.

They had converted the walk-in closet into another bedroom for Barb, and they had used the storage room as a place for her father's friends to sleep. Someone had left a radio on in that room, and the futon the kids had been sleeping on had disappeared with them.

This room smelled like pee, too, and Kara suspected it wasn't dog pee.

She shivered just a little and was about to leave when something about the radio announcer's voice caught her attention.

. . . repeat: the alien attacks have not ended. Stay in the cities. No one has issued an all clear yet. Stay where you are. Then the announcer's voice lowered as he continued. *We have received reports that the roads leading out of Chicago are clogged. Traffic is at a standstill on 90, 94, 290, 294 . . .*

He was giving the interstate names because most people were unfamiliar with the road systems here. Her father had explained that to Kara last month, when all the people poured in.

She felt a shiver run down her spine.

It wasn't over yet. This announcement was for real.

She ran through the sitting area and out the main door of the wing. The yard was empty. Plastic cups blew across it in the winter breeze. There were flat spots on the grass where the tents used to be.

All those people. People who had stayed with her. People she had gotten to know. They could die. Because they had left early.

She put her hands to her face. She would even miss those silly dogs.

If only she had heard this announcement earlier. If only they hadn't been so eager to return home.

If only.

She would have to tell her parents and warn the Hendricksons. And then they should try to reach her cousins and grandparents on their personal links, see if they could find a way back to the house. She wondered if anyone knew how to reach the Nelsons. She doubted it.

A buzzing above her made her look up, her heart in her throat. For a moment, she had been afraid the aliens were above her, but it wasn't them.

It was a small plane flying overhead, gray dust pouring out of it, the gray dust drifting and disappearing into the air.

November 12, 2018
4:30 P.M. Eastern Standard Time

Second Harvest: Third Day

Leo Cross had never dialed so many numbers and talked with so many people simultaneously. His office felt hot and crowded, even though he was the only person in it. All the screens were on, most of them blank now, and his desk unit hummed.

Adrenaline had kept him moving for the last two hours. Adrenaline and concern that the aliens had one more trick up their many tentacled sleeves.

If they even wore sleeves.

He had spoken to every nanotechnology expert he

could find. The only one who had been able to help him was, of course, Portia Groopman. She'd immediately seen the problem and searched for the solution. The others wanted to check and cross-check.

All Portia wanted was a chance to spend the night at Britt's apartment with her cats. Portia had been doing that a lot lately. Cross had a sense the girl was very lonely.

He hoped he would have a chance to help her meet some people her age, and find an apartment, and do all the things she had never had an opportunity to do.

But he wouldn't get that chance unless he succeeded now.

And he thought he could. He had the general's answer. He just had to let her know.

He pressed the screen in front of him, and turned away from the pop-up vid unit, not wanting to see the process as the phone described its every act. A holdover from the first computerized phones that Cross hadn't realized was so annoying, not until he saw it on the large screen.

The same man answered, and before Cross could say a word, the man put him on hold.

This time Cross glanced at the screen. It read "transferring . . ." He grinned. Apparently he had even more credibility with Maddox's staff now.

In less than a minute, Maddox appeared on the vid screen. This time she wasn't flattened or distorted. She was talking to him from an office. The walls behind her were black and he recognized the material. It was the same material that had been in the conference room where the final Tenth Planet Project meeting had been held.

"I have an answer for you," he said.

"Excellent." She leaned forward, waiting.

"Before I give it, I want to make sure—"

"Cross, we need it quickly."

"General," he said, "If we weren't communicating before, I'll be giving you the wrong information. Let me tell you what I thought you suggested so that we have no confusion."

"You should have checked that before," she said.

"I've been playing telephone with the most esoteric minds in the world. I want to make sure this stuff didn't get scrambled along the way."

"All right," she said. "Fire."

He nodded and said, "After the aliens drop their next harvesters, you want to roll projectile cannons into the areas. When the alien ships return for the harvesters and have their underbellies open, you want to fire into the ships."

"That's right," the general said. "Similar to how we attacked them with our planes in April, only these are a type of rail gun."

"Catapults," Cross said, holding his breath. That had been the term he had used with the nanotechnologists.

"In a word," the general said.

Cross had understood the problem completely. They couldn't fly planes near the ships, but if they could get under them, they could fire the same altitude-detonating bombs that the planes had dropped. It would be one last parting shot.

When the general had first called him, she had asked for ways of protecting weapons among the harvesters. Cross had had to pry all of this other information out of her.

Now he was glad he had.

He had asked his advisers how to protect the catapults—the rail guns. And they had answered him. Portia in more detail than the others.

"Okay," he said, "here's your answer. The nanorescuers would protect the rail guns if a number of things were done. First, the guns need metal wheels. Second, spray the rescuers onto every nook and cranny of the rail guns, and continue spraying as the machines are moved through the alien harvesters."

"Got it," Maddox said. Then she grinned. "You want me to repeat your instructions?"

"Only if you didn't understand them."

"Oh, I understand them," she said. "And they're actually something we can do. Thanks."

She cut the connection. He had no doubt she would spend the next fourteen hours staging rail guns and tanks of nanorescuers around the world, ready to move instantly if alien ships picked an area close. After the aliens picked their locations, she would have less than eighteen hours to move the guns into positions inside the attack areas.

A tough task. But if anyone could do it, it would be Maddox.

She clearly wasn't going to let those aliens get the best of her. Again.

November 13, 2018
2:30 A.M. Eastern Standard Time

Second Harvest: Fourth Day

Every time Clarissa Maddox came to the Oval Office she felt like a kid who was being sent to the principal. The very room itself commanded respect. And even though Franklin was as human as anyone— maybe more so, given his office—he seemed all the more powerful in this room.

Maybe that was why he had moved back here, even though there was going to be one more fight with the aliens.

Although his chief of staff, Grace Lopez, said the president had hightailed it out of the war room just before he had received the news of the return attack.

If he weren't her superior, and if he weren't so focused on the problems at hand, Maddox would have dressed him down. He was the symbol of leadership for the entire world. The last thing they needed was some fluke in which the alien attack took out Franklin, too.

When Maddox had arrived, the Oval Office had been filled with some of the president's closest advisers. Doug Mickelson, Shamus O'Grady, Grace Lopez, and others were on the couches, having a heated discussion about something. They all looked exhausted. The press secretary, Patrick Aldrich, was just leaving.

But when Franklin saw Maddox, he made a slight movement with his hand and apparently everyone knew that he had dismissed them. They had all left.

Maddox had been irritated by that because she was worried that she'd have to brief the president and then brief them. She didn't have a lot of time here. Coming up to the Oval Office had taken more time than she wanted to spend.

Of course, she couldn't say that to Franklin, but she was tempted. She was very tempted.

It took her less than three minutes to explain the catapult plan to Franklin. She gave him all the reasons why an attack from the ground just might work.

He had listened intently, his head bowed. Technically, he was supposed to consult with the other foreign leaders before he made any decisions, but she knew that whatever he said was going to happen. There wasn't time left for debate.

Which was why she was going to make one other suggestion, one she hadn't discussed with anyone, not her staff, not Cross, not anyone.

But it was one she thought would work.

"Mr. President," she said, clasping her hands behind her back, "the alien warships guarding the harvest ships are vulnerable in one other way."

Franklin's dark eyes narrowed. He'd worked with her enough that he knew when she used this tone she was extremely serious. "This is something I'm not going to like, isn't it?"

"Sir," she said, "let me respectfully submit we're past the point of having to like any plan that we choose to follow."

He turned away, lips pursed. "It *is* something I'm not going to like. Proceed, General."

She hated it when he did that. The feeling of having gone to the principal's office grew. "Our planes and rockets are always destroyed just half a kilometer away from the harvest ships and defense ships."

"You found some significance in that, didn't you?"

She nodded curtly. She wasn't going to let his skepticism or his exhaustion influence her. She was going to present this and then, if she could, browbeat him into accepting it.

"Mr. President," Maddox said, swallowing hard. "Shaped, directional nuclear charges, set off three quarters of a kilometer from an alien ship, would destroy the ship, or render it effectively useless."

"You and your nukes," he said.

She bit back a response. If he had let her use nukes the very first time, they might not be in this predicament.

Of course, the flip side of that scenario was that they were unfamiliar with the energy-stealing shield the aliens had, and the aliens might have neutralized the electronics in the nuclear weapons, but not the weapons themselves. It could have backfired badly.

This time it wouldn't. This time they knew what they were facing.

"What would your plan do to our atmosphere?"

It took her a moment to realize that Franklin's ques-

214

tion meant he was considering the plan. She worked hard at not looking startled.

"The explosions would be as 'clean' as we can make them, sir," she said. "The damage would be far less than the aliens will do to the ground under that ship by harvesting it."

Which meant, of course, that there would be damage. They both knew that. Franklin's dark gaze met hers. She could feel his intensity, the way he considered every point.

She was giving him a way to win this. She knew it. And so did he.

Finally, his gaze broke away from hers. "Are you suggesting, General, that we attack the alien ships as they come down, not allow them to drop their harvesters?"

"That's exactly what I am saying, sir," she said.

Franklin moved his head back as if he were arguing with himself. "We've already lost a lot of land and people to these creatures."

"Yes, sir." She let her resentment come out in both words. She hated losing anything to anyone. The aliens had gotten the better of her twice. It didn't matter that she had had victories of her own. She wouldn't be happy until those creatures were gone.

"If I authorize this," he said, "do we have time to notify every foreign government?"

"Yes, sir," Maddox said. "As long as you put someone like Mickelson on it."

To her surprise, Franklin grinned. "This is a task that's too big for Mickelson. I have a hunch I'll be placing those calls. We have to let our allies know we haven't lost our minds."

"Of course, sir."

Franklin's smile faded. "How many nukes are you planning to set off?"

This was the question she had hoped he wasn't going to ask. She squared her shoulders and took a deep breath. "They have over seventy ships left, sir. We'll fire one per ship, if we can get to them in time."

"Seventy," he said softly. And then he actually shuddered.

11

November 13, 2018
10:16 Universal Time

Second Harvest: Fourth Day

Technically, Commander Cicoi was supposed to listen to the Elder. He knew the Commanders of the North and Center were listening to theirs. But they had not promoted him to commander of the entire fleet, nor were they the ones who, by default, found the fate of their entire peoples in their hands.

If he spoke using the wasteful broadcast light, so that the others could see how his eyestalks swayed, the position of his tentacles, the way that he stood, then perhaps he might convince them to forsake the Elders.

But what if their Elders were giving them good advice?

What if his was?

His two damaged eyestalks throbbed so badly that he wanted to yank them out. He had already lost ships.

By his people's standards, he had failed again. He had nothing to lose by arguing with the Elder.

Besides, his plan, not the Elder's, had saved Malmur.

Cicoi's lower tentacles let go of the command center and he pulled himself out of the room with his upper tentacles. His staff turned their eyestalks away from him so they would not see him leave. He hadn't given them permission to look directly at him.

He did not put his Second in charge. They would have to contact him if they needed him. The time remaining until they had to go back to Malmur was crucial; he did not need an underling making the wrong decision.

Perhaps that was how the Elder felt. Not that it mattered. Cicoi would remind him that the Elder had been willing to let Malmur handle the incoming explosives by themselves. If they had followed the Elder's plan, instead of Cicoi's, half of Malmur would be damaged by now. The three ships that Cicoi had sent back had destroyed most of the explosives. The ships from the surface, with their inexperienced crews, had only taken out about a third.

Cicoi let himself into the privacy chamber. It was a small chamber, available only to officers, and it had not been used at all on this trip. But he felt that he had to be alone for a moment. He knew that the Elder wanted to speak to him, and Cicoi did not want a repeat of the scene from the last time. Cicoi's crew was too well trained to question him over his strange pantomimes and reactions, but there was no sense in letting them see that again—even if they did know that he was talking to the Elder.

He placed his lower tentacles on the relaxation circle, feeling the vibration ease his tensions. Then, just as quickly, he removed the tentacles. He did not need to relax. He needed to remain sharp. He still had work to do.

At least he had managed to harvest almost all the food they needed for the trip into the darkness. The food was stored in the bays of the harvest ships. It was time to return to Malmur and try to repair all the damage before they had to go into the long sleep.

That was what he would argue with the Elder. He knew the Elder would oppose that plan.

Because it is foolish and does not take into account our enemies.

The Elder had been inside his head. Cicoi would be glad when this trip was over, when the Elder returned to the Elders Circle or into the nether regions where time, it seemed, did not exist.

You should not be hostile to me, the Elder said.

Cicoi did not answer. There was no way to answer. He wasn't hostile to the Elder, not in the way the Elder thought. But he wasn't going to harm his own people for a gain that seemed false.

We shall attack the enemies below, the Elder said.

Their life spans are short, Cicoi thought. *The creatures we fight now will be long dead.*

They have a culture now, with space travel and marvelous weapons. They will have ways of keeping records. They will remember.

Cicoi felt the force of the Elder's belief.

Imagine, the Elder said, *if they expand as they have during the last sleep, how strong they will be. Perhaps they will have colonies on nearby planets. Perhaps they will have weapons to intercept us while we are still in cold sleep. Perhaps they will try to annihilate us before we enter their solar system.*

We can't prevent that now, Cicoi thought. *We must return to Malmur. We have enough food, and we have our ships. If we lose any more for your vengeance, we will harm ourselves even more.*

If we damage them heavily, the Elder said, *with their shortened life spans, we might be able to take away their technological achievements. They might spend many decaunits repairing what they have lost, and they might not be able to attack us again.*

Cicoi's eyestalks quivered. *You are basing a lot on supposition.*

The Elder formed in front of him. Solid darkness, so close that Cicoi could touch him if he wanted. The Elder's upper tentacles were wrapped around his torso. He was as uncertain about this as Cicoi.

Here is what I know, the Elder said. *If we do not attack them, they will have a plan for defeating us when we return. If we do attack them, we have a chance of damaging them. Perhaps they will not think it possible to harm us.*

If they were going to feel that way, Cicoi thought, *it would have happened during the first harvest. Instead they attacked us. Harming them now might provoke a more serious attack in the future.*

His own upper tentacles were wrapped around his torso. He was as uncertain as the Elder.

We must make some type of mark, the Elder said, *or they will believe that they may attack us and we will not retaliate.*

This last silenced Cicoi. On this most recent pass, the Malmuria had harvested and they had defended themselves, but they had not attacked. Were the creatures sophisticated enough to know the difference between a harvest and an attack?

Perhaps.

That was the gamble that the Elder was making. If the creatures were that sophisticated, they would prepare for Malmur's return, and perhaps try to destroy it completely.

The creatures had the benefit of light and darkness, growing plants, and a lush water-filled world. Malmur had that once and did no longer. It was stunting their growth.

They had to find a way to stunt the creatures', as well.

"The only way to harm them would be to decimate their population centers," Cicoi said.

That is what I was thinking, the Elder said. *But there are thousands of them.*

Cicoi had studied the globes that represented the third planet throughout his entire trip. He had learned something from them.

"There are large population centers," he said, "and there are smaller ones. We have already destroyed some of the smaller ones since they were near our harvest areas. I think we should choose the largest population centers. I suspect the repositories for their technologies will be in those places, as well."

Excellent, the Elder said. *Send the ships down. We shall—*

"No," Cicoi said, surprising himself. "We cannot send all of the ships down."

If we are to destroy the creatures—

"We cannot destroy all of the creatures. We can only show them our superior power."

You are afraid, the Elder said.

Cicoi turned his eight remaining eyestalks toward the Elder in direct defiance of tradition. "I am not afraid," he said. "I must guarantee my people's lives. You do not need food or energy or water. We do. We have already lost pods and nestlings. We have not revived entire sections on this Pass. All of the food we have gathered sits in these ships. We shall not risk it all for retaliation."

They will not know what we are doing. They—

"They have proven tremendously resourceful. If they have discovered a way to destroy ships—"

They would have done so by now. The Elder raised his upper tentacles, showing that he recognized and disapproved of Cicoi's rudeness. *Instead they tried to attack and we thwarted them. They do not have enough time to come up with a new plan.*

"We have underestimated them too many times," Cicoi said. He rose on his lower tentacles so that the Elder could continue to see his offensive eyestalks, pointing in the wrong direction. "I command this fleet, and I shall make the final determination. I agree with

222

you. We must attack them, but we shall do so with only half of our ships. If we lose them, we still have enough for starvation rations."

You are planning for failure.

Cicoi's upper tentacles wrapped so tightly around his torso that they would leave welts. Failure. That was the word for all of his command. Of course he was planning for failure.

He would be a fool not to.

"If you're wrong, and they destroy all of our ships," Cicoi said, as levelly as he could, "then our people die. If I'm wrong, and they destroy only half of our ships, then we have a future. You can call that planning for failure if you want. I think it sensible."

The Elder turned his own eyestalks toward Cicoi. It was an eerie look, for Cicoi couldn't see the eyes on the tips. Only darkness all the way up. *You will not change this decision, will you?*

Cicoi felt his upper tentacles loosen. The Elder was admitting that no matter what the decision, Cicoi would win. Cicoi was the only one of them who could command the crew.

"No," Cicoi said, not changing his physical position at all. "I will not."

The Elder let his eyestalks wilt, a sign of submission. Cicoi tried not to let his own eyestalks bulge in surprise.

Then, the Elder said. *I suggest we make one other change.*

Cicoi braced himself for another argument, but the Elder didn't seem to notice.

I suggest we divide the remaining ships into five harvesters, each guarded by a fighter. That will give us seven squads. We send each squad to a population center.

Cicoi's upper tentacles rose with excitement. This might work. "The creatures like to cluster," he said. "Five harvesters and all of their Sulas might be enough to take out all seven population centers."

The Elder's upper tentacles rose as well. *You approve of the plan?*

"If we have to attack," Cicoi said, "this is the best way to do it."

Then let us pick the centers, the Elder said, and headed out of the private room.

"I'll do that," Cicoi said. He wanted to maintain as much control as possible.

November 13, 2018
6:39 A.M. Eastern Standard Time

Second Harvest: Fourth Day

Maddox had just finished the last slice of cold pepperoni pizza. The gourmet chefs bunkered down with the staff were probably frustrated. Put a group of Americans under stress and they wanted junk food, not low-fat specialty foods made out of ingredients no one recognized.

The pizzas had come in about an hour ago. This was

the first chance Maddox had had to try a slice. Nothing tasted better than cold pepperoni, especially to someone as hungry as she was.

The war room looked extremely busy, and it felt like home. The patchwork hologram of Earth faced her like a battered child. She was going to defend it this time. She swore she was.

She picked up a can of Diet Coke and took a sip when Ward said, "Sir, the alien ships are breaking orbit."

She set the can down, knowing she would forget about it entirely in the next few minutes. She'd been lucky to get anything to eat at all.

"I need a visual," she said. By that, she meant she wanted the holographic representation. That had been working beautifully for her.

"Sir," said one of the techs down front, "only half of the ships are leaving orbit. And they're splitting up into seven groups."

The pizza Maddox had just finished churned in her stomach. Predictable, Cross had said. And if they weren't predictable, they sent a message with their changes. An unintentional message, but a message all the same.

She wasn't sure she liked the message she was getting. "You're sure about this?"

"Yes, sir."

She went to her own screen, touched it, and saw the same information. Seven of the fighters that had destroyed her planes were escorting the harvesting ships.

"I'm not getting a reading on directions," she said.

"Three groups coming toward the North American continent, two toward Asia, two toward Europe."

"Shit, shit, shit," she said, not as softly as she had hoped.

She looked up. The visuals were there. She could see how the ships were separating, how they were splitting into different directions. She mentally extended those directions onto a course, and tried to imagine what the aliens were aiming at.

It didn't take her long to figure it out.

"Cities!" she said. "They are going for major cities!"

Her staff was too well trained to react to that, but she knew how they were feeling.

She was feeling the same way. Frustrated and furious. Why couldn't those bastards play by the rules they had set up?

"Fighters are all standing by," Ward said. "Confirm launch orders?"

She touched the blinking red light on her screen, the one that was keyed to her fingerprint. A light extended from the screen, giving her a retinal scan. She did her best not to blink.

Then the link confirmed her, and within seconds, President Franklin's face appeared.

He looked years older than the last time she had seen him—and that had only been hours ago.

"Mr. President?" she said.

"I see what's happening, General." He was back in the war room beneath the White House. She wanted to kiss whoever had convinced him to go there. "Do you know what it is?"

"I believe they are going to attack cities, sir."

Franklin cursed loudly and creatively.

"My sentiments exactly, sir."

"Those nanorescuers had better work, Maddox."

As if she would be able to do anything if they didn't. "Yes, sir," she said. "But I'd rather not test them."

Franklin grinned. It was one of the nastiest looks she had ever seen on a human face.

"I agree, General," he said. "Blow them out of the sky."

"Understood, sir."

She turned to Ward. "Launch orders confirmed. All planes are ordered to attack when in range. All targets must be above twenty thousand feet. No lower."

She took a deep breath and then stood there, hands behind her back, waiting.

Watching.

At the moment, there was nothing more for her to do.

November 13, 2018
6:46 A.M. Eastern Standard Time

Second Harvest: Fourth Day

All the screens in Britt's lab were monitoring the alien ships. Satellites caught images of some of them. Others were being traced, in real time, by telemetry while someone—Cross had no idea who—translated that telemetry into real images.

On the main screen in the front of the room, Britt had asked for a large world map. On it, the trajectories of the alien ships were displayed.

Only half of the ships were coming down, but thirty-five were harvesters and seven were those fighters from before. They had split off and were going in seven different directions.

Britt was tracking them now. She and Cross had had the same idea: trace the trajectories and try to figure out where the ships were going.

Cross wanted to get up and pace, but the last time he had done that, he had made the entire team nervous. So he leaned on a desk and drummed his fingers on his legs, wishing he hadn't been right about the third attack.

But that was all he had been right about. He had thought that the third attack would have been like all the others: three groups over three different areas, largely using harvesting ships.

This change had him baffled.

He didn't like the feeling.

He also didn't like the way that the aliens had thrown away millennia of experience to adapt to Earth's attacks.

These aliens were a lot more flexible than he had given them credit for. He was glad they only had a short window for this next attack. If they had had time for a fourth, he wouldn't have known what to do.

"Leo." Britt spoke softly, but she caught the atten-

228

tion of everyone in the room. She was standing near her desk, her body hunched over it as if protecting anyone else from seeing what she had found.

He hurried to her side. On the screen was the same map of the world, only here the ships' trajectories had been plotted into a course with a probable destination.

Cities.

Of course.

Cross felt the breath leave his body.

London.

Moscow.

Beijing.

Seoul.

New York.

Los Angeles.

Chicago.

Son of a bitch.

It was as if they had maps of the major population centers of the world. Maybe they did. These creatures were resourceful, after all.

"This isn't a food run," Britt said softly. "This is a war retaliation run. They want to hurt us enough to make us leave them alone. And the only way to do that would be to hit our population centers."

Cross stared at the trajectories and suggested targets. They'd missed a lot, of course. Tokyo, Miami, Paris, Berlin. But the ones they'd chosen had been incredibly sound. They would destroy areas that would harm the world economy, as well as the areas themselves. And destroy seats of governments.

"Alien ships at sixty thousand and dropping," said

Odette Roosevelt. "Still no visual, but we should be picking up some shortly."

Cross looked up at the screens, but they still weren't showing much that he could understand.

Suddenly one screen burst into an intense white light, then went dark again.

"Was that us?" Britt asked, glancing around at her people. "Did one of the screens go?"

"No," someone said from the back of the room. "That was a visual."

"Of what?"

Cross felt the same question shudder through him. What had just happened?

Voices raised all over the lab.

People stood, and Cross could see hands working, touching screens and finessing work.

Britt bumped him out of the way and, with the touch of two fingers, got rid of the projected targets screens. Numbers poured across her desk, and while she might have understood them, Cross didn't.

Another screen flared white.

Then another, and another.

Cross felt himself grow cold.

Did the aliens have a way to bomb the cities from a higher elevation? Was he seeing the destruction of his own people?

The voices around him grew louder.

The normally contained scientists were shouting at each other for more information. Some of them stood on chairs to see the displays better.

Others were still bent over their desks, trying to figure out what was going on.

Britt was cursing under her breath.

Cross started to pace.

Another screen flared white.

The shouting in the room increased.

"That's it! That's it! *That's it!*" Britt shouted, clearly angry.

Her voice sounded shriller than Cross had ever heard it. She managed to shout her way through the noise.

Her staff quieted down. They all looked to her like unruly school children who had been caught misbehaving.

Cross looked at them and knew exactly how they all felt. They did look like children, but like children who wanted her to find a way to save them.

"You all have to calm down," Britt said. "We need answers and we need them fast. Others are depending on us. Now, figure out what's happening out there."

A few more screens flared white.

Then the same screens again.

Then more and more.

Cross quickly lost count.

"It seems," Roosevelt said, "that we are attacking and blowing up the alien ships."

"How?" Britt demanded.

Cross slapped the heel of his hand against his forehead. Of course. All those arguments long ago. "Maddox," he said with approval.

"What?" Britt turned on him. "You know what's going on?"

He grinned at her. He couldn't contain himself. The phrase "blowing up alien ships" was beginning to sink in. "I have an educated guess."

"Then educate the rest of us," Britt snapped.

"They're atomic charges," he said. "Shaped charges, aimed from a mile or so away at the alien ships. Nothing could withstand such a blast. It seems that General Maddox finally got to use her nukes."

Someone whistled behind him. "That explains my readings."

"And mine."

"Is that right?" Britt asked, glancing at her people, then back at Cross. "Are we destroying alien ships?"

"Well," Roosevelt said. "Something's exploding out there and it's not what's sending off those charges. They're hitting something. And correct me if I'm wrong, but we've seen a lot of technical wizardry for those aliens, but we ain't never seen no nukes."

"That's right," Cross said.

The screens were still flaring around them. Cross wanted to get closer, to see more, but he knew this was a battle being fought in skies far from him. Even if he went outside, he wouldn't be able to see anything. And if he were on the ground below the battles, the best thing he could do was be inside.

"How many alien ships have we destroyed so far?" Cross asked.

"It looks like half," Roosevelt said.

"Twenty," Britt said, looking at her own screen. "The rest are climbing back toward orbit."

"You're kidding," Cross said, staring at the monitor. It wasn't telling him anything.

"I'm not," Britt said. "The aliens are retreating. The ships in orbit are breaking out of orbit, headed for the tenth planet."

There was a moment of stunned silence around the room.

Cross had never felt anything like it before. It was as if every nerve in his body was about to explode.

Then everyone shouted at once.

Cross felt that silly grin he'd been wearing grow.

And grow. He hadn't felt like this—maybe ever.

Maybe he, too, had thought they were going to lose this battle.

He turned to Britt and gathered her in his arms.

She wrapped herself around him, pulling him close.

It was the best hug he had felt in his entire life.

And for some reason, neither of them wanted to let go of the other.

12

Second Harvest: Fourth Day

Commander Cicoi stood at his command center, his eyestalks floating free, his upper tentacles splayed on the center's controls. His lower tentacles were wrapped on the command circle, and he was forcing himself to stand as tall as possible.

He had failed, and he could not put himself into the recycler. He was fighting every bit of training he had ever had to keep himself here, in charge of what remained of the fleet.

If he had not stood up to the Elder, all of the harvester ships would have been destroyed. There would have been nothing left to feed his people.

If he had not stood up to the Elder, the explosives the creatures of the third planet had sent toward Malmur would have destroyed it.

He had succeeded as well. But not in the ways he

had planned. He had hoped to feed all his people, to defeat the creatures of the third planet, and to return home triumphant. Now he would have to defend himself and his leadership until the time for sleep.

The Elder had disappeared. As the strange explosives—similar in energy signature to the ones that had hit Malmur in that surprise attack—had destroyed ships, the Elder had slowly faded away. Cicoi kept expecting him to reappear, but he hadn't.

The Elder was smart enough to know that he had ordered this destruction. If he had led this command entirely, Malmur would be a dead planet, with the remains of a once great civilization.

As it was, the Malmuria would struggle with the greatest disaster they had faced since they lost their sun. Only it wasn't as great a disaster as it could have been.

And Cicoi had learned something else. The ancient knowledge was valuable. The Elders had ideas and weapons and experiences that he could never have.

But they did not understand modern Malmur. They had lived in a time of great wealth and privilege. Until this disaster, the Elder had not realized how fragile Malmur was.

And it was very fragile.

But it was also very strong.

Cicoi moved his first upper tentacle and checked on the fleet. They were heading home now, lighter than they had come. He had ordered the retreat because he knew they had no way of fighting the creatures' weapons.

The creatures were living through the same prolonged period of wealth the Elders had lived through.

236

The creatures had unlimited resources—or so it seemed—and the determination to use them.

Cicoi could not fight that.

So he had stopped trying.

He was limping home with sixty ships, more than half of the 108 he had started with. Enough, as he had said to the Elder, to feed his people starvation rations. Or to keep half of the population healthy, depending on the decision made by the Council.

Cicoi was not part of the Council and would not make that decision. He was glad of it. He had made too many decisions as it was.

Although he would argue for another, and he suspected he would win.

He was going to argue that recycling Commanders was not the way to cope with failure, not in a time of limited resources. For the Commanders learned from failure.

He had.

He had learned that the creatures of the third planet were as determined to protect their home as he was. He had also learned they would stop at nothing to do so.

It was a valuable lesson.

And one that had to survive the long sleep. For in addition to repairing Malmur, readying the ships for the next Pass, and preparing for the sleep, his people had another task.

They had to plan for the days when they faced the third planet again. To them, that day would come very, very soon.

Cicoi could only hope that the creatures of the third planet made the mistakes so many other sentient beings made. He would hope that they were no longer in existence when he returned.

But, seeing their determination and their resourcefulness, he doubted that would happen. He suspected his greatest fears would come true.

When he returned, after the long sleep, the creatures would have had countless generations to figure out how to fight the Malmuria. While the Malmuria slept and did not change, the creatures might grow in power just as they had in the last sleep.

Right now, they were capable of defending their home.

They might become capable of attacking his home while the cold sleep continued.

He had to prepare the leaders for that.

The long period of simple harvesting and sleeping had ended. The Malmuria were in a new period, one made up of war and struggle. The sooner they realized that, the better their chances for survival.

Cicoi was determined to be part of that survival.

He would not make the same mistakes in the future. Next time the creatures would not stand in his way. And he would not underestimate them again.

November 13, 2018
11:54 A.M. Eastern Standard Time

Second Harvest: Fourth Day

Leo Cross looked out the windows of Britt's apartment. The quiet neighborhood stretched before him.

Cars were moving as if it were a typical workday. People were outside, rebuilding, working on preparing for winter. Trying to resume their normal lives.

So quickly. So very quickly.

That told him that everyone missed the world as it had been.

Even though it would never be the same.

He turned. Britt's cat Muffin guarded the door to the kitchen. Cross was Muffin's arch enemy: he always took her time away from Britt. And Muffin was even more determined now than ever to have time with Britt. Muffin had no idea what had taken Britt from her these last few months, but Cross suspected that Muffin blamed him.

Interspecies communication didn't work on this planet. He wondered why he had ever thought he could comprehend a species from another planet.

He sat at the dining room table. He couldn't remember ever being this tired in his life. Part of the exhaustion was physical—he hadn't had more than eight hours of sleep total in the past week—but the bulk of his exhaustion, he knew, was relief.

There was no way the aliens would return in his lifetime. He would never see them or their ships again, never again view the tenth planet in real time.

Of course, its arrival, the war, the downed ships and the harvesters, as well as the few glimpses of the planet itself, would give scientists, researchers, and people like Cross enough work to last the rest of their lives.

"Did you microwave the potpies?" Britt asked as she

came into the room. Her other cat, Clyde, was following her like a lost puppy. The cats hadn't received much attention since the planet was discovered. They didn't know yet that they would have Britt with them more often.

Cross looked at Muffin who sat in front of the kitchen entry. "I value my shins too much to try."

"Well, frozen potpies aren't the best dinner, but it's what I have." She worked her way around Muffin, who followed her, purring, into the kitchen. Britt was humming. She was clearly as relieved as Cross, and probably even more tired.

After a moment, he heard the hum of the microwave. Britt came out with two apples and tossed him one. It was shiny and red, but he checked it for brown spots all the same. He had no idea when Britt had last had a chance to shop for food.

She sank into the chair across from him. He smiled at her. He'd been in the apartment a lot since he started working in the lab, but he hadn't been there with her. He couldn't remember the last time he had seen her in her own home.

"I feel like I should be working," she said.

"Me, too." He took a bite out of the apple. "We'll have plenty to do after we get some rest."

She nodded, then turned her apple over and over in her hands. "I keep thinking about that map of the world, the one with all the dark spots on it."

"All the people who died," Cross said softly.

Fifty million was the rough estimate. People who didn't understand the threat, like some of the native tribes in the Amazon; people who had refused to evacuate; and then the people who had fought against the aliens.

Fifty million out of a population of ten billion was statistically a huge success. But statistics weren't helping Cross.

Fifty million people, all of whom were known by someone, and probably loved by someone.

That was a lot of lives. A lot of lives lost to a war that no one had ever expected.

Too many lives for him to face comfortably. The relief work and the level of mourning worldwide was going to be huge.

"The people who died." Britt sounded reflective. She shook her head, and he recognized the movement. It was the one she made when she surprised herself. "You thought of the people who died. I was thinking about the food. We're going to have a lot of shortages, aren't we?"

"Not here," he said. "Once again, the United States lucked out. We were heading into spring the first time, and they only hit a section of California. This time, we're heading into winter, and the areas they hit in the U.S. were mostly forest. We'll have enough food. We'll probably have to go into full production for the first time in a hundred years so that we can meet the worldwide demand."

"Other places will starve then," she said.

"Africa. Parts of Europe." He set the apple down. It suddenly wasn't as appealing. "I don't know enough about the current economy of Central and South

America to know what the loss of the rain forests will do to them."

"How long?" Britt asked.

"Will they suffer?" He shrugged. "Depends on how the governments handle it. You've heard the reports. The dust that the nanoharvesters left is nontoxic. Stuff should be growing in it next spring."

"And the nukes?" she asked softly. "What about the fallout from them?"

She apparently hadn't believed Franklin's speech just an hour before about the "cleanliness" of the nuclear attack.

"The president was right," Cross said. "The radiation will circle the Earth for a few years, but compared to the damage that the aliens would have done—"

"That's minimizing, Leo." Britt rubbed her eyes with the back of her hand. "We're going to suffer something from it."

He nodded. "You know the drill, Britt. You don't need me to tell you."

"Increased cancers. Climate problems." She got up. "Those aliens have left us with a mess."

"It could have been a lot worse."

The microwave dinged in the kitchen. Britt went to get their food. The plan was to eat and then go to bed. To sleep. Cross doubted he had enough energy for anything else. They actually had time for that later.

All the time in the world.

He heard drawers open and a cat meow. Muffin and Clyde were probably circling Britt, hoping for treats.

During their brief meal, he had to get her to talk

242

about other things. He didn't want to talk about what was going to happen next. He wasn't sure he wanted to think about it.

There wasn't just the devastation, the loss of lives, the possible disasters worldwide, and the radiation threats. There were also questions that he had had from the beginning, questions about the new world that had been formed by the alliance between all the countries, by the martial law imposed, by the way the scientists had given away a lot of autonomy to the governments in the name of peace.

So many battles lay ahead. Human battles.

He suspected someone would sue over the nanorescuers, too. Since they never got to be used, and they dusted every major city, someone would see them as a threat. Even though they weren't. They were harmless to everything except the aliens' harvesters. In time, Portia assured him, they would break down into their component parts. *The cities will be dustier for a few years, that's all*, she had said, and he knew she was right.

Britt brought out steaming potpies. They weren't frozen food like he expected, but some from a local restaurant—or what had been a local restaurant until a few weeks ago. He wasn't even sure it had windows left, let alone equipment.

The smell of the chicken and sauce made his stomach growl. "How'd you get these?" he asked.

"You said to stock up on food," she said. "So I stocked up on stuff I knew we wouldn't get for a while."

He grinned at her. An impractical solution that had actually turned practical. If the world had ended, these potpies would never have lasted as long as the ones that were full of preservatives and fake vegetables.

He dug in.

"You're quiet," she said. "You don't want me to know how upset you are, do you?"

He looked at her. She was the only person he had ever met who completely understood him. It was a bit disconcerting at times.

"We've lost a lot," he said. "We probably don't even know yet all that's gone."

"At least the human race can get on with life again," Britt said.

"It won't work that way," Leo said.

"Why not?" Britt asked.

"Because we know they're out there."

"Yeah, but they'll be sleeping. Frozen for two thousand years. The ultimate cold war."

So she was going to get it out of him no matter what.

He sighed. "It won't make any difference," he said. "We still know they're there, and that information will eat at us until we do something about it."

Britt looked out the window at the afternoon sky, then shuddered. "What would we do?"

Cross chose not to look at the sky. Britt was smart. She'd figure out the options. There were only two of them. Either the human race got past this war and decided to share the planet with the aliens, or one of the races was going to be destroyed.

"We have time to figure out something," Cross said carefully. "And that's what bothers me the most."

November 13, 2018
5:12 P.M. Central Standard Time

Second Harvest: Fourth Day

Kara stood in front of the picture window in her now-empty home. Everyone was gone except her own family. The house suddenly seemed excessively large for three people.

Her father stood beside her, his arm around her, holding her close. They were watching the sunset.

It had an odd glow. It was redder, darker, gloomier than any sunset she had ever seen before. And a part of her didn't care. They had used nuclear bombs to save her city. She had seen the intense flash of light that seemed to fill every corner of everything, even inside the house. Then she had heard them explode overhead. The booms were tremendous, shaking everything.

But nothing would have been as bad as melting under those alien devices. No one had to test those nanorescuers. Everything was safe.

Although her mother was already talking about selling the house, and seeing if her father could move his law practice somewhere else. He had tried explaining to her that the radiation was in the Earth's atmosphere, and that everyone would be exposed, but she wasn't listening.

She never listened.

Kara leaned against her father. She'd take a world with extra radiation. She'd even take the spots some of her neighbors were seeing because they'd been outside during the blast.

She had looked down the well of having no future. Any future was better than that.

She would always remember that, the feeling of having no future.

She also understood now what it meant to choose between difficult things. If the president hadn't given the order to fire those nukes, her city might be gone.

She might be gone.

And she might never have seen this sunset, tainted though it was.

Her father hadn't said much. He didn't have to. The relief on his face told her everything she needed to know. She felt very secure against him.

Secure, knowing that she'd never see those aliens again in her lifetime. But she felt vulnerable, too. From now on, she wouldn't see the Earth as an isolated place, but as an island in space, vulnerable to attack.

An island that she was trapped on.

The strangely colored sun disappeared behind a line of black clouds. She squinted, trying to see beyond the orange glow on the horizon. Trying to see clear to the hated tenth planet. Soon, those aliens and their planet would be headed out into deep space, frozen. Yet every night, when she went out and looked up at the stars, she would remember they were out there.

She would remember that they had tried to kill her, and everything she knew and loved.

And she would remember they were coming back.

**Two thousand and six years
until the next harvest.**

THE 10TH PLANET

The ultimate battle for survival!

Bethesda Softworks cordially invites you to witness the next revolution in computer games as you join the desperate fight for humanity against the diabolical aliens of *The Tenth Planet*.

Featuring unparalleled 3D graphics, lush cutscenes, and intense action!!

In this fast, furious action game based on the suspenseful science fiction book *The Tenth Planet*, you'll take to the skies as part of an elite strike force sent to save the Earth from the alien onslaught. Battle high above the Earth in futuristic fighters. Feel the g's as you engage in tense dogfights against the never-before-seen alien fighter craft!

Using the latest in 3D technology, *The Tenth Planet* brings the epic struggle to your computer screen with exceptional graphics and detail that make you feel like you're really there.

Coming to a retailer near you!

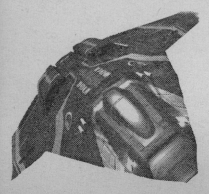

DEL REY® ONLINE!

The Del Rey Internet Newsletter...

A monthly electronic publication e-mailed to subscribers and posted on the rec.arts.sf.written Usenet newsgroup and on our Del Rey Books Web site (www.randomhouse.com/delrey/). It features hype-free descriptions of books that are new in the stores, a list of our upcoming books, special promotional programs and offers, announcements and news, a signing/reading/convention-attendance calendar for Del Rey authors and editors, "In Depth" essays in which professionals in the field (authors, artists, cover designers, salespeople, etc.) talk about their jobs in science fiction, a question-and-answer section, and more!

Subscribe to the DRIN: send a blank message to
join-drin-dist@list.randomhouse.com

The Del Rey Books Web Site!

We make a lot of information available on our Web site at
www.randomhouse.com/delrey/

- all back issues and the current issue of the Del Rey Internet Newsletter
- sample chapters of almost every new book
- detailed interactive features for some of our books
- special features on various authors and SF/F worlds
- reader reviews of some upcoming books
- news and announcements
- our Works in Progress report, detailing the doings of our most popular authors
- and more!

If You're Not on the Web...

You can subscribe to the DRIN via e-mail (send a blank message to join-drin-dist@list.randomhouse.com) or read it on the rec.arts.sf.written Usenet newsgroup the first few days of every month. We also have editors and other representatives who participate in America Online and CompuServe SF/F forums and rec.arts.sf.written, making contact and sharing information with SF/F readers.

Questions? E-mail us...

at delrey@randomhouse.com (though it sometimes takes us a little while to answer).